"Andy Mozina is a magician. I can't think of a species of masculine folly—whether guilty rebellion, or panicky narcissism, or dependency disguised as tyranny, or anomie passing as glib enthusiasm for new lines of an employer's tortilla chips—whose vocabulary and broken inner self Andy Mozina has not deftly conjured up for this collection. And he is as funny as he is wise."

■ JAIMY GORDON, National Book Award–winning author of *Lord of Misrule*

"Andy Mozina's dark comic midwestern genius thrills and troubles me, and I want more of it. Each of these stories is a philosophical puzzle, and each is a strange adventure to the foreign land that is another person's mind. Through his plainspoken narrators, Mozina takes us farther than we meant to go—to the edge of the Arctic Ocean, to Elvis's bedroom, to the terrible confusion at the heart of every human relationship. I love this collection."

■ BONNIE JO CAMPBELL, bestselling author of *Once Upon a River* and National Book Award finalist for *American Salvage* (Wayne State University Press, 2009)

"Andy Mozina's *Quality Snacks* is a collection of sad Rust Belt love songs. He maps a territory of dispirited office workers and aging small town beauties, all of them already beaten, always on the verge of worse. Echoes of Vonnegut, Borges, Cheever, and Saunders converge in these strip mall parking lots, in these dimly lit motels. Mozina asserts himself here as the fabulist poet of the Great Lakes working stiff."

■ TONY D'SOUZA, author of *Whiteman and Mule*

"It's a powerful effect, to wedge the sad into the funny, the strange into the normal in order to split a character (or world) apart, and it's one that I'm fond of. The oddness and commitment to the internal logic of these stories cements it: Mozina's creating his own worlds, in the same circles, maybe, as George Saunders' or Brock Clarke's, but distinctly his own."

■ ANDER MONSON, editor of the literary magazine *DIAGRAM* and author of *Vanishing Point*

Quality Snacks

Stories by Andy Mozina

WAYNE STATE UNIVERSITY PRESS | DETROIT

© 2014 by Wayne State University Press, Detroit, Michigan 48201.
All rights reserved. No part of this book may be reproduced without
formal permission. Manufactured in the United States of America.

18 17 16 15 14   5 4 3 2 1

ISBN 978-0-8143-4015-8 (paperback) / ISBN 978-0-8143-4016-5 (e-book)

Library of Congress Control Number: 2013954617

∞

Designed and typeset by Charlie Sharp, Sharp Des!gns, Lansing, Michigan
Composed in Pona

For Lorri

Contents

Dogs I Have Known

It is said that dogs are good. People with dogs live longer, are happier, and are less likely to have their homes burglarized.

I have never owned a dog. This is in part because I am afraid of them, but also because I do not want to take care of an animal. My daughter would love a dog, but I will never buy her one.

So I guess you know what kind of person I am.

ONE DOG'S NEIGHBORHOOD

The dog has his memories, a street where trees don't grow very tall. South Milwaukee. Small houses with complicated rooflines: dormers, additions, awnings, and porches. An air conditioner punched out a window like a Pez in mid-dispense. Gutters sag, downspouts dangle, shingles grow moss. Inside are staircases with hairpin curves, dining rooms with old built-ins, upstairs bedrooms with slanted ceilings, tiny closets shaped like mathematics problems.

One scrubbed kitchen smells from years of meat, a century of congealed gravy, coffee grounds, boiled spinach. A candy thermometer has fallen between the stove and the cupboard, visible with a flashlight but essentially lost forever. The backyard is exactly one-tenth the size of a football field, with a white Virgin Mary statue on a pile of stones at the fifty-yard line. The dog lived and barked and dished here, between white picket fences, his own classic wooden doghouse back-to-back with the garage on the alley.

Next door stands a corner tavern, also like a house, with the bar on the first floor and a family—my family—upstairs. Big square Pabst Blue Ribbon sign lit from within. A block over is the parish school, made out of the same rusty bricks as the foundry four streets away. Wedged into the complex like a gymnasium is a church with surprisingly beautiful stained-glass windows. Then there's the gymnasium itself, with its accordion bleachers and caged lights.

The dog was a nipper, yet loved by all. At first communions, he was always invited into the picture, sitting on his haunches by the girl in her white dress or the boy in his little suit. The pairing of child and dog gave the impression of an imaginary wedding in a children's game. I have such a Polaroid of Max, the dog, with Ginnie Lee, my first love.

Outside the school, the marquee reads: *Divine Mercy Catholic Parish. Excellence in Academics. Den of the Wildcats.*

MITCH AND SUSAN'S DOG

The closest I have come to being mauled and killed by a dog was at a Thanksgiving party thrown by my brother-in-law and his new wife.

It was a strange time for me. I had been experiencing a high level of conflict in the workplace. Even among other lawyers, my conversational style was deemed "excessively argumentative." The firm had been trying to promote collegiality among our attorneys, and it was felt that we needed to keep it down and respect each other and save our relentlessness for the courtroom and other venues where verbal sparring was the mode and expectation.

There was a particular set-to I had in a conference room with a colleague who was advocating, to my view, a manifestly losing strategy in a case she and I were on together. The problem occurred when she did not see something I felt was obviously apparent and true—and still think is obviously apparent and true. But she would not see it, and my voice rose and rose, and neither of us could stop. The managing partner personally escorted me to HR, where I was debriefed about my behavior, which was apparently part of a pattern. I was told that my style raised concerns, and I was put on a sort of probation, and the decision about whether I would be a partner was postponed.

My wife, Beth, did not appreciate this development, as she had convinced herself that my finally making partner would work a miraculous change for the better in the harried life we were leading in our three-story limestone-and-brick house on Wrightwood in west Lincoln Park, Chicago. In an effort to patch things up, she e-mailed the woman with whom I had argued. This woman responded with a volatile mix of truth and distortion, and as we discussed these matters in tense postdinner conversations, while our five-year-old daughter Amanda watched her Elmo movie, my wife began to wonder, it seemed to me, whether she had married a bad man.

We arrived early at the Thanksgiving party up in St. Charles. When I rang the bell, a dog's deep-throated bark exploded at a distant remove and then quickly grew louder, and then stopped growing louder, while still being very loud, because the dog was right behind the front door and for the moment could not get any closer. The barking was so forceful it agitated the innermost molecules of otherwise dense objects, like the porch slab under my feet. I stepped back, trying to position Beth and Amanda between the dog and me, because they were comfortable with all dogs at all times. Susan came to the door and said in a silly, joshing manner, "Oh, you stop it," to the dog, who growled as we stepped into the house. Something in the dog's growl made Susan reach down and grab its collar, which was a lucky thing for me because I was radiating the sort of acute fear that drives dogs berserk and makes them kill.

The dog was a German shepherd, thick across the shoulders, with a wolfish snout and wet black eyes. Its tail, I would say, swayed rather than wagged. During Susan's futile efforts to quiet its barking, I learned its name was Roxanne.

We amoebaed into the kitchen, where a spread of appetizers was laid out on an island: cold veggies and strange salads and even shrimp. Not many folks were there so far—Mitch and his brother Charlie were apparently out getting last-minute things—but I was glad to greet and hug anyone and so prove to Roxanne that I was a member of the pack in good standing. The dog kept coming back to me though, sniffing my crotch and growling. Then she stepped back and barked very loudly at me, baring her teeth.

"Hi, Roxanne," I said in a thin voice, standing with my hands at my sides, debating whether to extend the back of one for her to sniff and lick.

"Roxy, that's enough," Susan said. "There's drinks in the mudroom," she added.

"Do you want something?" I asked Beth. I was trying to be polite so she would not think I was a bad man.

"Sure," she said, without looking at me. "White wine."

I backed over to the mudroom and filled a wineglass sitting on top of the clothes dryer, then fished a Bud Light out of the utility sink. I twisted off the cap and drank the beer in less than a minute. My eyes watered. I opened another.

Carrying my second beer and Beth's wine, I returned to the kitchen. Roxanne was in the family room with the kids. Amanda was hugging Roxanne's neck from the side, and Roxanne was looking away like a cruel teenager. Amanda had been asking for a dog lately, and I had maintained my position despite some Category Five whining episodes.

"That's some dog," I said to Susan, who was basting an enormous golden-brown turkey.

"Brian is afraid of dogs," Beth told Susan, taking the glass of wine from me.

"I'm not afraid of dogs. I just don't think this dog knows me very well."

"She's a sweetheart," Susan said. "She's just protecting me because Mitch isn't here. She knows you're a male."

It was oddly reassuring to have my manhood affirmed by a dog, and for a moment I wondered if this was worth Roxanne's hostility.

Just as Mitch and Charlie walked in via the garage, the doorbell also rang, and Roxanne went nuts. It was Beth's folks and, right on their heels, two more of Beth's brothers and their families. Roxanne barked wildly, though now there was almost a recreational quality to it.

"Roxanne. *Roxy!*" Mitch said. "Settle down—now!" But the dog didn't mind him.

"Should I ask them to put the dog somewhere?" Beth asked me.

"Hey, Sis," Mitch said, and he embraced Beth.

"No," I said to Beth. "I wouldn't do that."

"Do what?" Mitch asked.

"Put the dog somewhere," Beth said. "She's scaring Brian."

"She'll be fine," Susan said, coming from the living room, an edge of exasperation in her voice. It was her dog and predated her marriage to Mitch. "She's just excited to see all the people."

"Hi, partner," Mitch said to me, extending his hand for a shake. I knew he meant "partner" in the Wild West sense and not in the law-firm sense. We shook, and then he leashed Roxanne and held her away from people. Roxanne leaped and strained and barked.

"Mitch, please take off the damn leash," Susan said sharply. "You're making her think something's wrong!"

I eased into the mudroom for another beer.

When dinner was served buffet-style, I hung back, even though I was incredibly hungry, because I didn't want to seem like an aggressive hog. By the time I filled my plate, all the seats in the kitchen had been taken, so I went into the dining room, where the table was extremely low to the floor and people were sitting on cushions, Japanese-style. Susan explained that she and Mitch had sawed off the legs of their dining room table because they liked the feel of sitting on the floor when they ate.

"It's neat," I said, even though I was sitting at the dog's level with an aromatic plate of meat and potatoes and gravy. I was drunk, but this had barely sanded the edges of my fear.

Then Roxanne swung into the room and circled the table; Susan had finally won the Battle of the Leash. I tried to ignore Roxanne until she nudged me under the armpit with her snout. I didn't know if she was trying to raise my arm so I could finally pet her and earn her trust, or if she was demanding that I hand her my plate. She could have bitten off my face without having to adjust her posture at all. Lifting my hand to pet her head seemed dangerous. I just kept eating and she kept nudging, until Mitch said, "Roxanne! Go sit down!" The dog considered him, then walked away.

Two of my sisters-in-law began arguing about how one of their children had been treated by a teacher. "I don't like the way she talked about Alex," the mom said. "And I had to take time off from work." The other sister-in-law, for various reasons, took the side of the teacher. As things got heated, the aggrieved mother asked for my opinion.

"Well, I see what both of you are saying," I offered. I very badly wanted to lie down.

When the dog came back, I impulsively rose from my cushion. "Excuse me," I said. I didn't have a plan, but I wandered through the kitchen, waved to Amanda at the kids' table in the family room, and turned down the front hall. I saw the pile of shoes near the door. If Roxanne had left my shoes uneaten, I would take a breather in the car.

Just as I was putting on my shoes, the dog came down the hall-way with her head and tail down—a common pre-attack attitude. I decided that my life was over and not a moment too soon. This produced a strange calm in me, and I said, "In case you haven't noticed, Roxy, I'm on my way out, so your little defend-the-house thing is going well."

My hands were trembling as I tied my laces. She put her muzzle to my fingers and growled her deepest growl.

But Mitch, who during his first marriage had become addicted to OxyContin but was now on his second marriage and pulling out of his tailspin in fine form, saw what was happening and called Roxanne to him, and she lifted her head and barked at me incredibly loudly. I straightened up, and as Mitch came for her, I opened the door and told Mitch that I needed air, which was true, and then I left the house.

I went to our car and moved the child seat to the front and lay down sideways on the backseat. I tried to fall asleep and make everything go away. But I couldn't sleep.

Maybe an hour or so later, Beth and Amanda came out. I sat up. In the same way that light is both a wave and a particle, my head swam and throbbed. Beth cut her eyes at me and made a dismissive hissing sound as she opened the passenger-side door. Amanda climbed into the backseat as I was heading out of it. "Hi, Daddy," she said. "What were you doing out here?"

"Taking a nap."

"I didn't know daddies take naps."

"Some daddies do," Beth said, moving Amanda's seat into the back.

After everyone was buckled, I rubbed my face with both hands and said to Beth, "How was it in there?"

"Oh, Mitch and Susan got into another fight about the dog."

"Sorry to hear that."

"Charlie and Fred were making fun of you."

"That's not right," I asserted.

MURRAY, MY FAVORITE DOG

From the moment I met him and he licked my hand, I knew Murray would never attack me, though he did doubt me once, which, for some people I have known, can be considered a form of attack. Still, he remains my favorite dog.

Murray was a Labradoodle who lived at my friend Frank's house in North Potomac, Maryland. He didn't shed. He rarely barked and never growled. He also sat by me sometimes in Frank's living room, and I petted his head and scratched his neck, while I drank wine and conversed freely with Frank and his wife, Rachel.

My friend Frank was a dark-haired, round, low-to-the-ground friend with whom I had gone to college. During that time, we had spent many a night getting drunk at parties and in the company of other friends, having boisterous conversations in which many things were hilarious and what we were heading for when we graduated could be ignored completely. My god, I loved those times! So after things degenerated and the divorce became final, and it was clear that Beth was never coming back, I took a trip to visit Frank as a way of rebuilding my happiness and self-esteem.

I have a tattoo of a labyrinth on my back, between the shoulder blades. It takes me two mirrors to see it and a lot of concentration to find my way out of it. I got it with Frank and some other guys during the week before graduation. I would never have predicted I would get a tattoo. But despite all the idiotic things I saw happen at my parents' bar, I loved to drink, and if you drink as regularly as I was drinking, eventually you will get at least one tattoo. Before passing out facedown on the tattooist's table, I did ask for the labyrinth, I'm pretty sure, but I don't remember asking for a Minotaur. Of course, when I look at it now, in two mirrors, the Minotaur doesn't look like anything so much as a large-headed dog.

As we were talking, we all got so drunk and relaxed that I told Frank and Rachel I had a tattoo of a labyrinth on my back and the labyrinth was guarded by none other than Murray. I pulled my shirt over my head and showed them. Frank laughed when he remembered, and Rachel told me I was "a troubled individual," but in a way that might have meant I was a fun guy and a good friend to Frank through the years.

Murray and I had only one awkward moment between us the entire visit: Frank and his son and I were walking Murray around their upscale suburban neighborhood of creeks and play lots and large colonial houses on cul-de-sacs. It was cool and drizzly, but for late December it was much more pleasant than the weather back in Chicago. At one point an SUV was parked at the end of a driveway, blocking the sidewalk. Frank, his son, and Murray went around the SUV to the left, going up the driveway. I went to the right, into the street, thinking this was more respectful to the homeowner. When I rejoined them, Murray confronted me. He sniffed me to discover who I was, as if he had never met me before. I slowed but did not stop, and Murray allowed me to continue with them.

Still, after my time with Murray, I actually reconsidered getting a dog. Beth had moved to an apartment in Bucktown so Amanda could stay in her Montessori school, and she hadn't bought a dog herself. Maybe I could prove Beth wrong about me and make Amanda happy during her three days a week at my place.

But then there would be the other days with me alone with the dog in the house. I could hear the tinkling of its tags as it approached, feel its warm breath on my knees, even through my pants. I would be reading the paper in a chair in the living room and the dog would make it clear to me that it wanted to be in that exact chair. What would I do? I have always counted on words to defend myself and my clients, to assert dominance as needed, but I could not imagine bearing the constant strain of having to assert dominance in my own home, and in a language I did not know how to speak.

REVENGE OF THE DOG

We all started barking, and our fascinating neighborhood enemy, John Nelson, retreated to his sandbox enclosure and methodically dug between his knees. We congregated on the basketball court of Divine Mercy, which was close to his lot line.

I turned to Ginnie Lee, my first love and next-door neighbor, and tried to kiss her ear, but it was a moving target. "Cut that out," she said.

She flattened her palms against her shorts and worked her tongue around her gums as if there were peanut butter on them. She had a boy's haircut, parted on the side. Her hair was black. She had large, adult breasts. We were thirteen.

How to go about being Ginnie's boyfriend was not clear to me. I didn't like hanging out at her house because of her dog. Once I talked to her from my bedroom window on the second floor above my family's bar, while she was in her yard with Max. She got down on her knees beside that dog and frolicked and wrestled with him. It was hard to hold a conversation that way. What if we became married and she wanted a dog?

Max, a smallish mutt, had almost been killed by Dozer, the Great Dane John Nelson's family had owned. Max had been loose on the sidewalk in front of the Lee home when John's father was out walking Dozer. In a flash, Dozer took Max in his mouth and shook him by the neck. Mr. Nelson held Dozer's leash but could not call off Dozer. Ginnie herself had broken Dozer's grip by beating the dog with a broom. A few months later, Dozer was hit by a car and killed.

We had been barking at John Nelson to taunt him with the loss of his malicious pooch, and, though I could taste my own cruelty in my metallic saliva, I barked the loudest because I was trying to please Ginnie and because I knew my imitation of Dozer's bark was uncannily close. Still kneeling in the sandbox, John Nelson finally unearthed a coffee can, opened it, and reached inside. His long bowl haircut swayed as he rose to his feet, holding what I was pretty sure was an M-80. He pulled his prized Zippo lighter from his T-shirt pocket and disappeared behind an overgrown bush at his property line.

Someone swished a basketball through the chain netting. When John stepped back into view, the long, customized fuse of his M-80 was burning.

My gut filled with butterflies.

"Eat me!" John yelled, and he hurled his bomb toward the basketball court.

Mesmerized, I stood and watched while the others scattered. Ginnie screamed.

The M-80 landed; I calculated ten seconds left on the fuse. Very conscious of Ginnie watching me, I did what any boy who had seen *The Dirty Dozen* would do: I reached for the M-80 to throw it back.

Even as I bent to grab it, wild emergency shouting went off in my blood. Nevertheless, I picked up the M-80. The sparking hiss sounded like something essential leaking from my head. I realized I was wrong about how much time was left; I spastically shoveled the M-80 into the air. It arced toward Ginnie, who shrieked. I heard the lightning crack, and Ginnie convulsed and reeled.

I ran to her quickly. She was bleeding from her ear. There were powder burns on the side of her face. She looked at me with her mouth open, but no sound was coming out. I thought the blast had deafened me, and in fact it had temporarily because as my hearing came back, I heard Ginnie's hard breathing more and more clearly.

"You idiot!" she shouted. "I can't hear, I can't hear!" She began crying.

"Get away from her!" her best friend, Luann Rodgers, yelled at me. She pushed me from the side, and I staggered for about fifteen feet, trying to keep my balance, before I finally went down and skinned my hands on the crumbling asphalt. Couldn't she tell it was an accident? Getting up, I found that everything was slow and cottony. There were some thick minutes when maybe I blacked out on my feet, shouting horrible things at Luann. When she stopped yelling back, I detected an echo from the surrounding houses.

"Where's John?" I asked, my voice hoarse, but no one answered me.

Then Ginnie's mother showed up on a ten-speed, which was odd, so I thought for sure I was dreaming and tried to wake up. She got off the bike and let it fall. I heard Max barking in the distance. I could picture his front paws up on the picket fence; I could tell when he got down and ran the fence and then got back up again.

Mrs. Lee went to Ginnie, who was still crying, and checked her wounds, and then wheeled and said, "What are you kids doing out here? Are you crazy?"

"John Nelson threw it," my brother Scott said. Scott was quite a ladies' man, and I thought his word would carry the situation.

"Not either!" Luann said. "Brian threw it."

"I said I was sorry!" I protested, though I don't think I had said it. Then I ran home because I was afraid I'd start to cry in front of everyone.

A week later I was sitting on the steps of the tavern when Ginnie came home with her mom. As Ginnie got out of the car, she wouldn't look at me, but I saw her beige hearing aid. It was like seeing Farrah Fawcett with a hearing aid.

I never got used to it. I hoped she would come to see John Nelson as the evil one. But, as a lawyer would say, I was the proximate cause of her hearing loss. In fact, near the end of eighth grade, she actually dated John. I kept my distance, waiting for her to come back to me.

I remember a definitive day on the playground. We were in our respective boy/girl gangs, standing around telling funny stories, and I looked over and saw Ginnie going on about something to her friends. She turned toward me and shouted, "Why can't you be like your brother? You are such a fucking loser!"

I stared at her across the playground, but nothing I wanted to say to her could be conveyed at that distance.

THE DOGS OF THE DOW

Having lost my wife and, eventually, my bid for partner and subsequently my job, I searched the important aspects of human experience for new terms by which I could judge myself A-OK. I came up with two. One of them was money: I had more money than most other people in the world, and if I could secure another job, the amount of money I had would continue to grow. The other was trying to make myself a better person. It is said that money and soul-improving activities don't mix, but for me they did: when I failed at being a better person, I could fall back on having money. This in turn gave me the strength I needed to renew my attempts to be a better person.

Karen, a law school friend who hated the swagger of litigators and everything they stood for, took pity on me and invited me into her mediation practice.

"Are you sure?" I asked at the Hard Rock Café in downtown Chicago. It was an idiotic place to have lunch, but it was my idea. "I tend to create conflict, not resolve it."

"But that's what will make you so good!" she enthused. "You really *understand* how conflict happens."

Karen's hair had gone gray when she was in her twenties. She had just let it happen. Later, it would occur to me that she used her long gray hair and her young face and willowy figure to work her mediatory magic, as if she were saying, give in to gray hair and death, mediate with it, and you'll be rewarded with cheerful willowiness.

She was having a salad; I was having a bacon cheeseburger. It was like one of those folktales where the bunny and the wolf end up good friends. I really wanted to date her, but she told me, apropos of what I don't remember, that her relationship with her boyfriend was "unusually strong." In fact, when the check came, she added, "My relationship with my boyfriend has recently grown stronger."

I am not good at seeing or hearing myself. The thing that helps people know how they're coming across to other people doesn't work very well in me. It's one of the reasons I fear dogs: because they might see what I don't want to show. To this day, I have no idea what I did to make Karen say those things to me.

When I was signing for the bill, Hendrix's version of "All Along the Watchtower" was playing. It happens to be my favorite song. It seemed clear during his trippy, funky guitar solo that I would mediate and have stronger relationships and become a better person. And also make money.

Unfortunately, as it turned out, my weakness as a mediator was a tendency toward excitable clarity. I would be a gentle listener until I grasped what I thought was going on; then, inevitably, my framing of what I saw would tick someone off. It wasn't long before I was back at another firm, this one specializing in insurance defense work, once again litigating my ass off.

In the meantime, I had been diligently pursuing my first goal, investing my money according to a strategy called "The Dogs of the Dow."

Take the five Dow Jones Industrial Average stocks with the worst performance the previous year and invest in them for the coming year. Hold for one year and then sell and invest in the five worst from the preceding year, and so on.

The idea, in a nutshell, is to profit from the fear of others.

SELDOM KNOWN FACTS ABOUT DOGS

Without ever seeming to look, a dog knows where its master's hands are at all times.

The nose of a dog is two thousand times more sensitive than the nose of a human.

Dogs make excellent earthquake detectors; they perceive the electromagnetic waves earthquakes emit just before they occur. If your dog acts erratically without apparent cause, release it from your home and follow it to safety.

When a dog barks, the semantic content is always, "There are things I wish to say. There are things I wish to say." There are no other "words" in dog language. All differential shades of meaning in dog communication come from the tone in which this desire to communicate is announced.

RUFUS

Though I was litigating again, I never abandoned my dream of becoming a better person. Even after I jumped ship, Karen sent me some pro bono work for a local hospice, and when the hospice director mentioned a volunteer drive, I said, "Count me in."

The volunteer training sessions were awkward. We were asked why we'd volunteered, and for all of the other trainees—a few in their thirties, some recently widowed—death had recently been a major part of their lives. Many of them had relatives who had been cared for by the hospice program, and they wanted to give something back. I felt like an imposter. Except for two pairs of grandparents whom I hardly knew, I had never been close to someone who had died; my well-pickled parents were chugging along, notwithstanding decades of first- and second-hand smoke. When it was my turn, I told the group, "I don't think we'll make it if we don't help each other once in a while."

I'm not sure how my rationale was received since I could not meet anyone's eyes and the silence that ensued was perfectly rippleless.

After we completed our training, I was assigned to Wilbur Tesch, former farmer, US marine, and hardware store manager, a man slowly dying from a pulmonary disorder. About once a week, I would provide respite for his wife, Caroline, so she could run errands for a few hours. Wilbur had asked for a man, and there were not a lot of male hospice volunteers.

Mr. Tesch lived in Cicero, a largely treeless expanse of low-rise, low-grade urbanicity whose residents had thrown things at Martin Luther King Jr. when he brought his civil rights movement north. I pulled up in front of the small Tesch home, which crowded the sidewalk the way small homes crowd sidewalks in South Milwaukee.

Caroline greeted me and invited me inside. In a cage in the kitchen was a dark brown muscular dog. He barked vigorously. "He's just a big baby," Caroline told me. "His name is Rufus."

"Hi, Rufus," I said.

Rufus was newly acquired to protect Caroline from prowlers when Wilbur finally passed. He was lean yet gave the sense of filling the cage.

"I just took him out," Caroline said. "You don't have to worry about that."

The way she said this let me know that Marigene, the volunteer coordinator, had passed on the gist of the note I had scrawled on the back of my volunteer questionnaire.

Wilbur was watching *The Price Is Right* in a brown leather recliner in the small family room at the rear of the house. He was wearing oxygen tubes. His left arm trembled. Still, he rose and shook my right hand firmly. Though his arms were mottled with wine-colored bruises and his ankles were swollen and chafed, he didn't seem as if he were about to die. Caroline showed me the backup generator for his oxygen if the power went out, gave me a tour of the refrigerator, and took off.

Wilbur wore a hearing aid and the TV was on quite loud, but he dampened the volume so we could talk. At times we watched the action on *The Price Is Right*, and at times I asked him a question, such as, "So what was your commanding officer like?"

Wilbur considered my questions as thoughtfully as I have ever seen anyone consider questions. "I'm trying to remember," he'd say in his airless voice. And when he did remember, he'd give a twenty-minute answer. Finally, he asked, "Do you want something to eat?"

When I walked into the kitchen to get out the food, Rufus didn't lunge at me or bark or get up or make any noise at all. I was almost disappointed.

Wilbur shuffled over to join me at the dining room table. He had an ice-cream bar, and I had a ham sandwich washed down with a caffeine-free Diet Pepsi.

After lunch, we repaired to the family room for more TV.

"You like hunting and fishing?" Wilbur asked.

"Yes," I said, automatically. "Very much." I had never hunted in my life and had only fished once for bluegill off a pier at Fries Lake in Wisconsin when I was a kid.

He fumbled with the remote and the channels clicked by. He passed CNBC and I saw the stock ticker running across the bottom. INTC, one of the dogs, was up thirty-nine cents. Not bad.

Wilbur settled on the Outdoor channel. We watched a pair of men hunt caribou in a highland meadow. They whispered excitedly as ten or twelve animals blundered into range, some inadvertently saving their lives by wandering behind a bush, others exposing themselves by trotting after a herd mate. At the key moment, the guide blew on some sort of kazoo, which froze all the caribou, and the hunter fired. One animal tensed for a millisecond and then bounded away, but apparently it was hit. The two men tracked the wounded caribou and found it dead in a ravine. They lifted its head by the rack.

"He's beautiful," the hunter said reverently. The caribou's neck had retained its flexibility: though it was lying flat on its side, the men were able to hold the head up straight by the antlers.

"That's a helluva animal," the guide said. He described the points on the rack in great detail. "A nice trophy," he concluded.

The hunter gave a big hand clasp to the guide and said, "Thank you so much." Then he added, with tremulous emotion, "This is awesome! A dream come true!"

"Pretty impressive," I said, though I was vaguely disturbed. The hospice had taught us never to upset a patient with our own beliefs. The hunter reminded me of being happy to learn Dozer was dead. It occurred to me, and not for the first time, that if I weren't afraid of dogs, I wouldn't have had anything to prove by barking and going for the M-80, and then Ginnie and I would have married, instead of Beth and I, and we would still be married.

While we were watching fishermen in a johnboat on what looked like a drainage ditch in Florida, Wilbur's son Henry showed up. Henry was a fit, straight-backed man with a mustache and thick graying hair. Wilbur had told me his son had fought in Vietnam. "Now he works for a woman," Wilbur had said with a sad disbelieving laugh.

Henry chatted with us for a bit, while Rufus whined to be let out.

QUALITY SNACKS / 20

"Time to release the beast," Henry said, and he stepped into the kitchen.

"You need some help?" I said as I stood up.

"He doesn't need help," Wilbur said.

Nevertheless, I went into the dining room, just in time to see Rufus drag Henry out the kitchen door. Henry clicked off the leash, and Rufus darted into the small backyard like a released fish. He did his business, then gamboled and turned and looked expectantly to Henry, his short tail wagging furiously. Henry picked up a chew stick and tossed it, and Rufus ran after it and brought it to him. I should have gone back to sit with Wilbur, but I couldn't take my eyes off the two of them. They played fetch for a while; then the next time Rufus brought back the stick, Henry grabbed it on either side of Rufus's jaw and waggled it. They played tug-of-war, man and dog, Henry and Rufus, rolling and playing, bumping into an empty blue kiddie pool on the grass, until they almost seemed of the same species and Rufus gave up the stick to Henry.

Rufus waited for Henry to throw the stick, but Henry lay on his back with his eyes closed and his arms over his head, looking exhausted by more than dog wrestling. Rufus approached and licked his face, and Henry smiled faintly, lying there for another ten seconds before he got up.

.   .   .

The following week the hospice nurse came and before I knew it she let Rufus out and filled his pool with a hose because it was a hot day, and the week after that, Caroline came back early. Then there was a day when it all went as the first day, and Wilbur and I were watching TV while his oxygen supply system motored and hissed and made occasional clicking and whumping sounds. During a fishing program, Rufus began to whine intermittently, and by the time a reindeer-hunting program came on, Rufus was whining piteously and continuously to be let out. His whine was high-pitched, loud, coercive; it shredded my consciousness. I rubbed my damp palms on my knees. I thought Wilbur might turn to me at any second and say, "Could you please let him out?" Instead, Wilbur repeatedly tried to shush Rufus, but the dog's whining found an extra gear, an even sharper pitch.

"No!" Wilbur finally shouted, though he was dangerously short of breath. "No!" He rose from his chair, his left arm shaking, his fist curled around a phantom newspaper. He almost toppled as he turned laboriously toward the kitchen, his oxygen tube dangling, his right hand braced on the armrest. If I were to help him, I would have to open the cage and quickly move my hand past Rufus's jaw to grasp his collar. I would speak soothingly while I did this and pray that whatever it was that gave me away to people wouldn't give me away to Rufus. I would let him drag me outside. I would let him go. Wilbur straightened and shuffled six feet to the kitchen doorway. It took him a full minute, the dog whining frantically. "No!" Wilbur hoarsely shouted. "No!"

Wilbur tottered. I sprang from the sofa and dashed to him. He tipped in my direction. I went to one knee, as if fielding a grounder, and took his falling weight against my shoulder. But he was heavier than I thought, and I sprawled backward, and Wilbur collapsed onto me, his foul-smelling hair tickling my nose, his pointy elbow sharply pinching the skin on the side of my midsection. "Ack!" he wheezed, lying on top of me, waving an arm; the tube stretching to his nose piece came loose. For a confused instant, I thought of Rufus and Henry wrestling in the backyard, and I imagined I was roughhousing with Wilbur in a similar way. But then I came to my senses.

MEDITATIVE DOG

Dogs circle me in fluorescent moonlight, in some rectangular South Milwaukee backyard. Their unruly loping. Their narrow mouths and oversize teeth. The thing I would never do, the thing I am afraid of, barks at me. I have the ability to hear dogs barking at great distances, in any weather. Every dog confirms for me that I am not near it.

You might expect that I would have had a case involving a dog. When a dog bites someone—and this happens with fair frequency, though never to me—a lawsuit sometimes ensues. But, given my largely corporate practice, I have never come across a case in which a dog's behavior was material. I have never even defended a corporation that breeds or distributes or caters to dogs. Nevertheless, sometimes I think dogs have taught me everything I know, that they have made me the man, and the litigator, I am today.

My daughter is ten now and she calls occasionally to renew her pleas. I tell her, if your mother can handle a dog at her apartment, I won't stop her, but I can't have a dog over here.

"Dad, you hate me," Amanda says.

"No, I don't, sweetie," I say. "I love you."

We hang up with something between us, I'm afraid.

Wilbur is of course dead now, but how did things turn out with Rufus? Did I ever wrestle with him in the backyard? Did I ever fill his pool with water? Did we play fetch? He was purebred Doberman, a beautiful dog, trust me. Once, I simply put the back of my right hand against his cage, and he licked my fingers through the bars.

Soon I will take profits in Pfizer, Boeing, and Intel and put the money into inflation-indexed treasuries. The dogs have had their run. My strategy has proved successful. It is time to turn somewhat conservative.

Pelvis

In his house, there are beautiful things. In the Jungle Room, there are statues of monkeys and a waterfall. In the Pool Room, there is a twist of tapestry for a ceiling. There is red and gold everywhere. He himself is a work of beauty—sideburn, lip, pelvis. What's known as a human god. Above men, though with them. Born among us, however different. He brings the heavens down to earth, down to his satin sheets. And I am a bit of the heavens to him.

The King wants me, and in his desire is my chance. But for what? Maybe the one-in-a-hundred chance the Pill will fail. (They made me prove I was taking the Pill; I have signed forms giving up rights against the King, which seems right for them, but as for me, I recognize no right offered or kept under any but the condition of true loving and the going down in feeling, where both get at it and make with it.) And I might have his child. His only beloved son. To be in this world, from my womb, through my loins.

But what should I want?

I have not opened my legs for any man. I am twenty-one years of age and I have had my chances. Very few women save themselves anymore. I do not blame them—there are too many reasons. I also had my reasons. But now, when I measure out my reasons, they do not touch my yearnings: I am complete and untouched for him and ready to be by him. That is all I need to know.

In the upstairs hallway, there are six women on seven metal folding chairs. And I would like to know, what is the right ratio between King and person? And what is the degree of virginity he truly wants and needs? Because I can tell that some of these women do not have enough. I can hear them saying, "It doesn't count," but we know. I can almost see the hinges in their hips, in the corners of their sarcastic smiles.

Still, I like to think that we seven are all virgins. People say he likes virgins. Seven per night when he is not out of town. All seven in some way, though it may take fourteen to sixteen hours. That's what we talk about, if we talk. How he has treated other women. But we have no sure way of knowing, now do we? But all of us, and feeling it, we can still tell ourselves stories of how it's been for other women with him, even as, and I know this, we all think of ourselves as the one for him, the one he'll remember and want to marry.

"I heard he's . . . I heard it's not so big," says one of them, blonde.

"You can say 'cock,'" says another, a redhead.

"Shush."

"Don't say it," a second blonde says.

"You women are weird to be squeamish."

"It's dignity."

"This is dignity?"

"You're not a virgin."

"Oh yes I am."

"Your attitude—"

"Is why I'm here."

"If he finds out you're not a virgin . . ."

"He'll do something," says the second blonde.

"He'll send us all home," the first blonde says, eyeing her friend and nodding, but now it seems like a routine the blondes are doing for each other. And suddenly I know: they will go in together.

"Don't worry, girls," the redhead says. "I'll bleed. Believe me."

"He won't know the difference," I say spitefully.

They all look daggers at me. I cannot please the King, I worry, but in my failure to please him I will know that he and I are not the same person and I am bringing myself to him from a separate world and he cannot completely have me.

We seven, counting the one in there now, we seven represent the continents. I am the continent of America and I recognize no other. I have come by bus though I have the money to fly. I have the money to fly because I work for a living in the United States.

Billy Zip is a boy I used to love and now undate every Saturday night when we don't go out. Billy Zip is a zero. Is a nothing. In the city of Milwaukee, on Forty-Third Street, against a Harnischfeger building, with beer on his breath, he touched what only Elvis must touch. He wrecked the zipper of my winter coat, opened it from the bottom, and his hands coming up my sweater touched my warm belly. The ice. My scream had a cloud to it.

You ain't no friend of mine, I said, in my mind. If only he knew his unfriendliness. If only he knew which side of the song to be on—the side of needing but not getting, of being frustrated but respectful. The side Elvis himself sings so well. I ran away from him, and he chased me down Forty-Third Street. I got across National because I wasn't afraid of the cars. I ran to the other side of Forty-Third Street—they got brakes. I was running from all of those factories, machine shops, ball-bearing plants. The five-story factories with big walls of windows made of small windows, and the concrete first story, and the employees' entrance in some obscure wall.

I kept running down Forty-Third Street and then kept walking until I was looking into County Stadium from way behind the center-field bleachers. I walked down the hill. I wandered the parking lot, crazy as a loon. And nearby were the spirits of great men. Here all the men did their best and the people cheered. There was my job—secretary. If a company is a body, then the secretary is a—it was exactly what I knew. I had seen this. I knew it was just a matter of time before one of them got to me. And I'd end up in a duplex on Fortieth Street, so his walk to work would be short, and so for his bar: Pip's, Irene's, Bindy's, Gene's, Dave's, Dale's, Dee's, The Happy Tap, The Cellar, The Attic, The Cave, Vince and Dottie's Christmas Tree Inn, Cookie's Tap Room, George's Unit Bar, Bill's Overtime Tap, The Corner Pocket, The Back Door, The Second Shift, The Starlight, The Peppermill, The Schoolhouse. Neon beer signs between the concrete and brick factories and the wood and aluminum flats. It was time to devote myself, before he got me, whoever he was, and made me open my legs and then it would be all over.

No, it will never be over. I save money religiously. I never spend it. I always want to have as much money as possible. So I can be on my own if I need to. And this is how we see that this is what it is: the King's money shows what he does for us, and my money shows what I can do for me. If necessary. And this is what being on my own really means: to be with the other women, and still yet to be by myself in his beautiful house. Rehearsing things to say in my head: "I believe you are a person, Mr. Presley. I believe that entitles you to my love, and so your love can come to me, if it would, out of you. Us, as people, giving and getting what is known as love, sung into our one brain of need by you yourself, have to go down and make this thing together, right now, as people, for the magic to be what we want to feel later, when you'll be the King again."

The door opens. The first girl steps out in a jumpsuit and big hoop earrings. She tilts her head so her blonde hair falls over her face, but then we can see the dark roots where the hair that will always be coming out of her is coming out still. A small man in an off-white leisure suit with large patch pockets leaves his post farther down the hall. He's holding a transistor radio to the side of his head. He meets her and she takes his elbow. He winks as they go by, whispers, "Ali, TKO, in the fifteenth." He bluffs an uppercut with his radio hand. I can almost smell his shiny black shoes through the cloud of our mingled perfumes. I can almost smell the leather case on the radio, which, to each of us—and I know this—broadcasts some different message from where we come from, for just a second. And then, in the next second, but just for a second, we all think of what the man, Ali, needs.

I have told myself that I have thought of the needs of men too many times in too many ways. I have seen the bra burners and I have fingered their literature. There is time to consider what the magazines are saying. There are worlds opening that were never open before, just as there are legs that must never open and legs that will open, still, I have no doubt, despite everything, and I think, is this it, is this the way with Mr. Presley? Is this the way? But when a man sings a beautiful song, and is who he is, who among us can resist in the name of a new principle? The strong can resist and the rest of us go down in loving flames, in hunks of burning love, in between what happened and what will happen.

(The man told us through the gate, He'll be home tonight, come on in, let's have a look at you.)

By way of good-bye, the redhead before me rises to her feet. She adjusts the ankle strap on one of her spiked heels and minces forward. And I'm afraid her mind is blank, because she's not thinking of what to do with this. She's just happening to herself, not even with the King, though he hips between her open legs. Who can be a redhead? Who can be a blonde and a brunette and a redhead?

So to save money religiously I took the bus from Milwaukee to Memphis, to have a go at the King. The only man who's worth it. The only man who would be worthy of ruining me and dragging me down.

But don't you know, Miss Redhead, that to be prepared in your mind is all that everything depends on if it's something you want to live on? So when I kiss him, it will be to kiss that man who waits for me at a pool table at a bar on Greenfield Avenue, in the shadow of Allis-Chalmers and Rexnord and Briggs & Stratton and the P&H Harnischfeger Corporation, at the south side of the valley that splits the city of Milwaukee and takes train tracks across its soft belly, south of where the freeway goes, south of Pigsville, south of the Miller Brewery, south of County Stadium where the teams of men play. And when I kiss the King, it will be so I can kiss that man later with a mouth made by King kisses and by my imagination into the mouth I had and always will have. The legs I got and will have. The opened legs. And I know that all of them are men, and only men, when the two are naked and the woman opens her legs. And I choose among men, with a man, how it makes a value I can live by. And I will bring the King's value with me, because I will have made it with him, with my own hands and body, my own imaginary hands, body, when I finally lay my true husband down.

Overpass

When Jack stepped off the city bus, wind blew into his open coat, drying his sweaty shirt and chilling him. The ride home from high school often made him motion sick, but there was nothing he could do about it, just as there was nothing he could do about the high school itself, which was large and old, with tall corridors that always seemed underlit. He zipped up his coat, licked the pimple at the corner of his mouth, and started home.

Before he had gone very far, he heard a voice yelling at him, calling him a pussy. It was his friend Stan, riding down the middle of the street on a ten-speed. Stan was coming right at him, playing chicken, but Jack was tired and couldn't make himself care. He stood his ground. Stan veered away at the last second, banked his bike in a tight circle and yelled again, this time with more respect, "Jack, you asshole!"

"Stan the man," Jack said, "lives in a garbage can, shits in the palm of his hand, sells it at the Popsicle stand."

Stan laughed, with a hard grin and electrified eyes. His hair was long and frizzed out. He was wearing a Boone's Farm T-shirt under an army jacket. He stopped his bike next to Jack and they high-fived.

"Where you been, dude?" Stan said.

"I don't know," Jack said.

"Man, you missed paint bombing St. Seb's."

Stan went on about all the vandalism, shoplifting, and sneaking out at night Jack had missed that summer. Jack hadn't seen Stan since eighth-grade graduation. It was late October now, and he was at St. Ignatius while Stan was doing ninth grade at Lane Junior High. The summer had been shot because Jack's mom had gone on a rampage about his grades. She had decided he should no longer hang out with Stan because Stan was going to end up in prison. Instead, she had held summer school for Jack, assigning algebra, compositions, piano practice. Once when he had complained, she had screamed at him for twenty minutes, lifting the ironing board a few inches off the floor and slamming it down, over and over.

"We should do something one of these days," Stan said, "like the old days."

"Yeah, I guess."

"Like tonight, before it gets too cold."

"Yeah, maybe."

Stan kept coming at him, circling him like a boxer, peppering him with how great it'd be to do something. Finally Jack agreed to meet Stan under the overpass, at 1:00 A.M., for drinking. Stan promised to bring everything. All Jack had to do was show up with cash for his half.

As Stan rode away no-handed, Jack knew this was a bad idea. Not only would his mom kill him if she found out, but he had to wake up early to make the lunches and catch the fucking bus. He would call Stan after dinner—maybe with the dishwasher running, so his mom wouldn't hear—and say he couldn't make it. Still, seeing Stan made him feel better.

When he got home, he saw his mom's Buick parked at a crazy angle, halfway up the driveway. He knew he was supposed to notice this. When summer ended, her mood had changed. She had been mostly in bed for three weeks now, but he wouldn't put it past her to drive out near the bus stop to spy on him walking home.

As soon as he walked in the door, her strained voice called from the bedroom, "Jack, come here."

The air in her room tasted damp and used. On a low table at the foot of the bed, next to the blank TV, the humidifier percolated softly and blew out steam. The nightstand was covered with medicines—little bottles and pill canisters. His mother lay propped up on three pillows. Her dyed brown hair was in curls, which she had permed herself with her Toni kit. When Jack was younger he used to help her with her home perms by spritzing the tightly wound curlers with the special chemical, or pulling the curlers open when the hair was set. It had been weird to see her white scalp.

"It's been an extremely difficult day," she said now, her voice a low, scratchy monotone. "I'm sure Sandra needs changing. Your aunt was over earlier, but she hates diapers. I had to run out—myself—and get a prescription your father forgot. Don't ever get married, Jack. It'll kill you." Her chin was on her chest, but she looked up to make steady eye contact, her mouth curved in a tired smile.

Jack tried to make sense of this look, which was both forbidding and a little playful.

She reached for something on her nightstand but knocked over a glass of water, which landed just hard enough to shatter on the worn gray carpet. She fell back.

"Darn it! What's the matter with me?"

Jack went for a plastic cup of water as well as a broom and dustpan to clean up the broken glass. When he came back, he swept up the wet shards, while she breathed loudly through her nose, as though asleep. He ground up two aspirin in a tablespoon and left it for her near the water because she was afraid of choking on pills. As he was about to leave, she said, "Check your father's room for laundry, but I don't want you starting a load. I'm going to get up and do the wash tomorrow, if I feel better."

Jack passed by the kitchen, where Arnie and Jeffrey were eating peanut butter by the spoonful right out of the jar.

"Hey, fellas," Jack said, stopping in the doorway.

"Hey, Dad," Arnie said, and he cracked up laughing.

Jack stood staring at his little brother.

"Come on, Arnie," Jeffrey said, eyes on Jack.

"Later, Pops," Arnie said, darting away.

Jack reached for him and Arnie squealed.

"Jack!" their mother managed to yell.

Jack let Arnie go and headed for the girls' room. The shades had been pulled, and the room was sunk in gray light. A dusty mobile of cardboard kitchen appliances—refrigerator, stove, toaster oven, dishwasher—twisted above Sandra's crib by the window. Sandra stood at the bars of her crib, snot crusted around her tiny nose. Her wail was weak, as if she had stopped expecting it to work. Cathleen was wide awake, lying in bed on the other side of the room.

He picked up Sandra and took her over to the changing table. He cleaned out her nose with an eyedropper and wiped it with a towelette. Sandra waved her legs and threw her arms forward. He peeled the diaper away from her legs and butt—it was loaded—and folded it like a burrito, which he retaped and threw in the trash. Lifting her by the ankles with his left hand, he wiped her thoroughly;

then he rubbed on some A&D ointment with one finger where she was red and put on a fresh diaper.

"She cried all day," Cathleen said.

He got Cathleen some apple juice and gave Sandra a bottle, then took Cathleen and Sandra into the living room. He handed the girls off to Arnie and told Jeffrey to vacuum the tiny bits of glass left around Mom's nightstand and then to set the table while he made spaghetti again.

.   .   .

His father came home on time. He was a trust officer at Marine Bank and rarely worked late. He burst into the kitchen through the back door, put his briefcase and a grocery bag on the counter, and said, "How's my right hand man?"

"Pretty good," Jack said.

His dad came over to inspect the burbling spaghetti sauce. "Let me taste," he said, opening his mouth. His moist red lips were rimmed with a new salt-and-pepper beard. As Jack put a spoonful in his dad's mouth, he could see the pink tongue swell up to meet the food.

"Not bad, Champ, not bad," his father said after swallowing. He pulled a bottle of wine out of the bag. "Try some oregano. We have garlic powder, don't we? Try that."

"Warren?" Jack's mother called.

"Open this for me, will you?" His father went to the sickroom.

The first thing Jack clearly overheard was his father's rising voice: "I said I was sorry!" He thought the argument would be worse, but the yelling died down abruptly.

Jack's father came back to the kitchen, uncorked his wine, drank off a glass. Then he stepped over to the stove where Jack was adding oregano to the sauce.

"The woman is not physically sick," he said in a low voice. He took a deep breath. "Look at yourself. You could be out playing ball, doing things with your pals after school, and you're stuck here running this house."

"It's OK," Jack said.

"Hey, I'm not criticizing you, you understand? I think you're doing a great job. I know what you're doing is hard, and it's not your fault."

Jack thought for a second. "What's not my fault?"

"Nothing—you're fine. You're all right. Listen, what can you do? You know?"

"No, I don't." Jack found himself laughing.

Jack's dad laughed too. "Hey, *I* don't know what I'm saying. I got to get out of this monkey suit before I lose my mind." He left his briefcase on the counter but picked up his wine. On his way out of the kitchen, he called back, "You're doing great. Keep up the good work."

.　　.　　.

At the end of the meal, Jack's father stood up and began clearing the table. "Boys," he said to Arnie and Jeffrey, "Jack is tired. You guys are on dish duty. I'll help."

Jack was caught off guard. It was as if something he'd been pushing on had suddenly been pulled away. "I can do it, Dad," he said.

"I know you can, Champ," his father said, lifting Sandra out of her high chair. "Take her."

Jack took Sandra. Jeffrey and Arnie got out of their chairs and started clearing the table. Cathleen ran away, heading for the TV.

He wandered to the bedroom he shared with Arnie and Jeffrey. Sandra kept trying to lunge from his arms, so he put her down to gum the football cards and army men and Matchbox cars and the other crap that cluttered the floor. He opened his junk drawer and dug up his Budweiser lighter, which he had shoplifted with Stan maybe a year ago. It was shaped like a little Budweiser can, but with a shiny veneer that made it pleasant to hold. He remembered walking the railroad tracks behind Colder's Warehouse Furniture with Stan and Tim and Bill, smoking cigarettes, the lighter fat in the back pocket of his jeans. He rolled the lighter in his hands for a bit, then buried it in his other junk.

He wanted to go tonight but only if he also had the option of not going. It was a strange feeling. Sandra started crying. He picked her up, and she cried harder. He didn't know why.

"You'll feel better in ten seconds!" he said, cradling her in his arms. "Ten, nine, eight . . ." He counted down so dramatically—giving her a little bounce with each number—that Sandra quieted, looked at him intently, and tried to put her thumb in his mouth. He saw his father walk by in the hallway, wearing his silver-and-black tracksuit and clutching hand weights, going out for his walk. Arnie and Jeffrey squealed in the kitchen. It sounded as if they were trying to spray each other with the hose attachment on the sink. The dishwasher wasn't running yet. Water would be all over the floor.

By the time he reached "one," he knew he wouldn't call Stan. He knew he would go.

.   .   .

The clock radio flipped to 12:30 A.M. Arnie and Jeffrey were breathing on the bunk beds across the room. Jack crept out of bed, took his jeans off the chair, and pulled them on. His hands were cold against his legs. He walked into the dim corridor, past his father's room—his old room—into the kitchen. Moonlight cut across the kitchen table.

"Jack?" his mother called from her bedroom. His upper body clenched. For a second he felt caught, but doing what? He was just standing in the kitchen.

He went down the corridor. The moonlight didn't shine in her room, and his eyes had to adjust to the darkness.

"Are you all right?" he heard himself say.

"The humidifier, I think it's running low on water."

The old humidifier had been handed down from his grandparents. He carried it to the bathroom, took it apart, and filled up the warm, brown, glass jar in the tub. Sometimes his mother watched the steam rise out of it. Did she see shapes, fantasies, dead relatives? He brought the humidifier back and plugged in the cloth cord. Maybe she just liked the sound of the steam, like the sound of wind through a loose window. Maybe to her it was like the sound of a man breathing.

He said good night and moved to the door.

"Jack?" she said.

He stopped. "Are you all right?" he said, wanting to get it over with—whatever it was.

"When I was a little girl . . ."

He'd stand there, but he wouldn't be there. She would say things to him, but it wouldn't matter. He was going to see Stan.

"When I was a little girl, I—"

"You were never a little girl, Mom. You've always been in bed. You've always been sick."

"I used to read books to you, even before you were born."

"I got to go back to sleep."

"Don't go. Tell me a story."

"I don't know any. Your throat sounds bad. Do you want some NyQuil?"

"Jack, do your friends at school believe in God?"

"It's a Catholic school, Mom." He stood by the doorway, dreading her next question: "Do you believe?" He didn't think he did.

He found the plastic measuring cup for the NyQuil on the nightstand. He poured some out for her. "Here, have some. So you can feel better."

"What is that? NyQuil?"

She took the cup like a little girl.

"Another," she said. "At this time of night . . ."

The NyQuil would only make her sleep. He poured another too high and spilled some. He was afraid his hand would shake. She drank the second cupful.

"Oh, you're good to me," she said. "Give me a hug."

When he bent over her, the heat from her bedclothes rose and mingled with the stale, sweaty smell hovering around her face and neck. Her breath was very sour. Her cheek was dry and soft.

"Good night," he said, slipping out of her arms. He backed out the door.

"Jack?"

He froze, listening.

"Just stay for a bit."

"I got to get up tomorrow," he whispered.

He edged down the hall. She gave a loud sigh, but then nothing. He went to the bathroom, as if that's why he'd gotten up in the first place, flushed the toilet, and headed to his room. Without going inside, he opened and closed the door, letting the catch make the loud click she would be listening for over the sound of the old toilet refilling, but then he managed to get down the carpeted hall to the kitchen before the noise of the tank had finished. Carefully controlling his breath, he stood near the sink for fifteen minutes, waiting for the NyQuil to take effect. Finally he heard her snores. He went to the back door, opened it, slipped out.

The air smelled like burning leaves. The moon lit motionless clouds. He realized he had gone out without shoes or a coat. He couldn't risk going back. He stole across the back sidewalk and into the garage. On a nail hung his father's old leather jacket and below sat a pair of work boots. He slipped on the stiff jacket. The boots fit loosely; a pocket of cold air surrounded his toes. He loped down the driveway, across the street, and through the Hacketts' yard. Once he made it to the field, he ran parallel with the freeway fence. The freeway was to his left, at the top of an incline, brightly lit like a stage. He passed a small clump of trees on his right and saw the broad, blackened stump where he and Stan used to torch army men and toads and tin cans and anything else that was too weak or too inanimate to escape their will to burn it.

At the far side of the field, a creek and a road passed side by side under a freeway overpass. Here the fence turned up the incline and stopped where the overpass began. Jack climbed up to the guardrail for the bridge. He ducked under the overpass and, crouching to avoid I beams, scrambled along a three-foot-wide shelf to the right of which the cement sloped steeply down to the creek. In a slot of light created by the gap between the eastbound and westbound lanes sat Stan.

"There's the motherfucker," Stan said, smiling and pointing at him with a can of Coke. A tall bottle of Cutty Sark stood on the cement. "I started without you."

Stan offered his cold, bony hand, and Jack shook it, hooking thumbs with Stan.

"I'll catch up," Jack said. He insisted on paying for all the Coke and the Sark. His dad had made a big deal about upping his allowance for the extra chores, and he never had a chance to spend the money.

Jack popped open a Coke and drank off as much as he could. He let Stan spike it.

"You sneak out OK?"

"I think so." Jack took a long drink, and the alcohol warmed his throat. "It's just good to get out of there."

What sounded like a pair of trucks rumbled overhead. Jack thrilled to the creaking of the I beams, the peculiar underwater quality of the sound. They concentrated on their drinks for a while. Jack added more Sark to his Coke. Stan pushed some sand down the cement slope.

"I feel kind of guilty sneaking out on my mom like this," Jack said, and he tested his new drink, which was strong.

Stan didn't answer, so Jack felt he had to add something tougher. "I'm not fucking having kids, that's for sure. Parents fucking hate kids. That's what's wrong with everything."

"Nah," Stan said. "Parents fucking hate each other. Sometimes they like their kids." Stan smiled without opening his lips.

"Too damn true," Jack said. But sitting there with Stan, the fact that parents hated each other was suddenly all right.

"Hey, we could use the magical armchair," Stan said, patting the cold, gritty concrete.

In seventh grade they had borrowed some shovels from the back porch of the convent and dug into the huge snowbank piled up at one end of the playground. They'd made a main cave and branching tunnels. One recess they found an armchair and a bunch of empty beer cans in the cave.

"There's *no* fucking way that chair could have fit through the opening," Stan said.

"A miracle," Jack said, though he knew the chair probably could have fit.

"And Mr. Balsa—'At the count of three, I want everyone out of this snowbank!'"

Stan laughed, and then Jack did, too. They couldn't get enough of that moment: Mr. Balsa, the pudgy music teacher with the orange beard, standing on the snow pile—right over their heads!—counting to three with the other kids on the playground clustered in front of him.

And then of course no one came out.

"At the count of three!" had become one of their favorite inside jokes.

.   .   .

Half an hour later, Jack's face and stomach hurt from laughing.

"Stan, I really miss you, man. I miss the shit we pulled."

"Fuck it. We can still pull shit. We're pulling shit right now. Am I right?" Stan got to his feet. "Come on, get up."

Stan looked up to the gap of light above their heads. With both hands he reached the insides of the median walls. He found a foothold and climbed up.

When Jack rose to his feet, he felt a sharp dizziness. He had to grab an I beam to keep from pitching down the slope. The world had grown very small. It seemed they had been there for days. He felt great, unbelievably drunk; he wanted to be able to do this always—get blotto with his friend Stan.

"Come on up, motherfucker!" Stan called down.

"I'm coming," Jack said. He found ledges and footholds, and he climbed, surprised his body knew how to move.

Jack emerged between the two low concrete median walls. Wind and sound swirled around the freeway, and the lights on the poles dazzled. A car swished by.

"What if the cops see us?" Jack said.

Stan threw a leg over the low wall. The next car beeped and he ignored it.

"What're we doing?" Jack said. From his room, he could see the freeway, but now here he was.

"All right," Stan said. "After the next car, we gotta run over to the right lane and do ten push-ups."

"Why?" Jack yelled, and flapped the oversize sleeves of his father's coat. He could imagine his mother wide-awake, trying to see the humidifier's steam, trying, maybe, to see Jack's shape. From where she lay, she could hear the same cars and trucks that rushed past him now. His father was probably faceup in Jack's old twin bed, snoring through his new beard. Everything in the world was next to everything else, at some distance. This idea amazed him.

"Come on." Stan pulled Jack's arm, and they ran across two westbound lanes and hit the pavement on the third. The concrete was cold, with little grooves for channeling water. Jack's arms trembled. The first push-up he miscalculated and bashed his forehead. The last nine amounted to bobbing his head up and down as quickly as he could, his heart racing: every sound of the wind was the sound of a car. They finished and bailed off the shoulder.

"Jesus Christ!" Jack shouted. He crawled over to where Stan was lying facing the road, as if they were pinned down by enemy machine gun fire. A car whizzed by.

Stan hawked up some phlegm, spat, said nothing. There was no fear in his face. His upper lip was flaring; his breath steamed out in puffs. It must have gotten colder while they were under the bridge. His eyes were wide, as if he were watching a movie from the first row.

The long grass, swirled by the wind, was clotted with trash. Jack tossed away an empty bottle of Jim Beam that had been digging into his gut. He breathed onto his cold hands. His temples beat loudly.

"Come on, let's go back out there," Stan said.

"To do what?" Jack laughed.

"Now we got to get a car to change lanes."

"What?"

"Yeah, listen. It's not dangerous at all. I mean, if you saw a big pile of shit in the middle of the road, wouldn't you change lanes?"

"I don't know, Stan." An image of Sandra crawling across the freeway flashed through his mind.

"Don't be a chicken."

"You go first."

"No, we do it side by side, buddies for life."

Jack wanted Stan to look at him. He thought they should shake hands first if it was going to make them buddies for life. But Stan kept looking away wide-eyed. Still, what was a handshake compared to what Stan was asking him to do?

"All right," Jack said. "All right, after this truck."

Over the crest of the hill appeared the headlights of a car. They darted out and then lay down on their stomachs side by side in the center lane, facing the direction the car was headed.

Jack heard the growing rush of the approaching car.

"Oh my God," Jack whispered. A strange, hiccuping laugh escaped him.

At the last second Stan yelled, "Don't move. They're going to swerve!"

The car shot past. It didn't even beep. They sat up; another car was only about seventy-five yards away. They yelled and rolled off into the weeds. That car beeped loudly.

"Jesus H. Christ, Jesus H. Christ," Jack gibbered. He had never heard his heart so loudly in his head. He was beyond drunk. This was the greatest thing he'd ever done. Buddies for life—he liked the idea. Fuck his parents, and fuck that house. As soon as he could, he was moving out. He and Stan and maybe Bill and Tim would get their own apartment. They'd party and relax like normal people. He turned on his back and looked up at the sky—a sheet of clouds stretched toward the sinking moon. The weeds around him spun. The dizziness made his stomach tighten. He rolled facedown, and the spinning slowed. Now it was a partial-spin-and-revolve-back motion, like the plastic fins in the washing machine did when they stirred the clothes.

"Three times," Stan was saying. "For the count of three. We got to go three times."

The cars came too fast. It wasn't like crossing the street. They were just *there*. Stan's face was right by Jack's. "Come on, keep moving or you'll pass out." It sounded as though he and Stan were in a room, maybe the kitchen at Jack's house, and Jack was holding Sandra at the kitchen table, his parents sitting across from him with their heads bowed, as if they were all in church, and then Stan was saying the same thing: keep moving or you'll pass out.

"Listen, listen!" Now Stan was so close to his ear it felt as if he were in Jack's head. "That car wasn't even freaked out—didn't know we were people. That's why we got to get them to change lanes *while* we're doing push-ups, so they can see we're moving—get it?"

"I don't know," Jack said. He thought he was going to throw up. He took some very large breaths and belched.

"Keep moving!"

Jack stood up and stepped into the breakdown lane. He remembered his father leaving the house in his tracksuit and his mother knocking over the glass.

"Come on," Stan said, getting down on his knees for his ten push-ups. He had overrun the right lane, so now he was pointing from the center lane into the right lane at an angle.

"We can't be in two places at once," Jack said, though maybe not loud enough for Stan to hear. He wanted to be home in his old bed, his old room, and he wanted to be on the freeway with Stan. He felt he was no place at all.

When he checked for cars, two were coming over the rise, one in the right lane and one in the center. Jack yelled out, the two cars arrived quickly, the one in the right lane trying to veer left but sliding. The other car sideswiped the median, making a grinding sound like a snowplow blade, sending up sparks. With its front wheel, the car in the right lane ran over Stan's back, and its skidding rear wheel pinched his shoulder and dragged him. Stan's arms were outstretched, but his head was skittering.

Jack staggered toward the cars. He smelled burned rubber. A man in an overcoat bounded out of the car that had run over Stan. Two women came out of the other car. Doors slammed. The man said, "No," and then one of the women screamed. She had climbed up on the median wall and pressed her hands together under her chin, like the statue of a saint. The other woman stepped toward Stan. The woman on the median yelled, "Get out of the road!"

"What is this?" the man said loudly, as if he wanted everyone to witness his reaction. "I don't believe this." He sounded more confused than upset.

Stan must be dead, Jack thought. The man in the overcoat knelt and bent over Stan, then stood up, raised his hands, and slapped them down against his sides. Steam came out of the man's mouth. Steam came out of the mouths of the women. Steam came out of Jack himself, though no one noticed. It seemed that, at any second, the woman and the man near Stan would comfort each other, and then everything would be all right.

A car pulled to the shoulder behind Jack. Other cars were arriving and stopping. Everyone kept breathing. Each cloud of breath was shaped differently, like a voice. The wind would let the breath hang before blowing it away. Buddies for life. He thought of his mother, and the shape of her breath was like a circle that got bigger and bigger until he was inside it.

Proofreader

I had turned to James, one of my proofreaders, to guide me in matters of love, to keep me from making mistakes. This now itself seemed to have been a mistake. On top of this, his work had begun to suffer.

So I called the jackal on the phone and ordered him over to my office, where he might not be so comfortable, where I might pull his forearm hair or pinch him with my staple remover. But when he was actually sitting in front of my glass desk, he said he was having blepharospasms and asked to use the washroom. His left eyelid was winking spastically.

"No," I said. "Relax. It'll pass."

He sat back in his chair, stared at my phone.

"Look at yourself," I said.

James did. He pulled his striped shirt away from his chest with thumb and forefinger. He looked over his knees, at his scuffed loafers. I could see them myself, beneath my glass desk.

"What do you see?" I asked.

He looked up at me, his eyelid twitching still. "A fuckup?"

"You're looking at me."

"Isn't that my job?" He seemed about to smile. "To keep you from making—?"

"Forget about it," I said. "We'll pay for it. *You* made a mistake. You wouldn't get up and open a goddamn dictionary, and now we have to pay to fix the film at the printers. Fine. What are you laughing at?"

It was barely a smirk, but as if to prove me correct, it puffed into a quick, coughing laugh. He said, "It was only one word, two letters."

"You're a goddamn proofreader!"

"Chief, we both know your real issue here." He relaxed in his chair. His poise infuriated me. "I've been talking to Joan."

"Does she know you're going to be fired?" I asked, and the more I thought my face might be blushing, the more I could feel it blush.

Joan works in the Art Department. The previous Saturday afternoon, she and I had gone for a walk along the Charles, from the B.U. Bridge to the Harvard boathouse, and then back to her apartment on Trowbridge Street.

"She talks to me," he said.

"What is it with you two?"

"We're friends." He said this like it was something I would never understand. Like I had never had a single true friend.

"What'd she say about me?"

"Really, not that much. Not that much you shouldn't already know."

"What's with your eye?" I asked, though the spasms had stopped. I thought that in order to regain my advantage I would have to get them going again. His spastic eye reminded me of my own tendency to become very dizzy while thinking about things that are very important to me yet are in severe doubt—things that demand immediate resolution yet appear resolvable only after long and uncertain effort.

"Chief, really, I—"

"Why do I listen to you?"

"You trust me." His smirk came back. "You're not yourself right now."

"What'd she say?"

"When?" He grinned sheepishly, lifted his palms. "When?"

I stretched my forearms onto my blotter. "Tell me what she said about me. Say it. Let me know." I karate-chopped the desk. I fixed him with my stare. I heard myself breathing through my nose.

"You probably don't want to know now," James said, and he raised his hand over his mouth, as if he might burst out laughing.

Despite the fact that a nontemporary romantic relationship had been my primary goal in life for more than twenty years, I had failed to achieve it. But the more I let James get involved in these matters, the more out of control things became.

"If you don't tell me . . . ," I started—but I couldn't formulate a credible threat.

After the walk, Joan and I had decided to go out to dinner at this Chinese place in Harvard Square. It was a spur of the moment decision. She'd proven a fast walker and we'd worked up a sweat. She invited me up to her apartment to shower and change. I could wear a pair of her jeans and a T-shirt, she said. I thought I could just as easily go home and change and meet her, but this was a promising sign, and James had said she liked spontaneity. I wanted her in the abstract, I know that for sure. Her appearance, her accomplishments, her toothy smile. She had been a ballet dancer and knew four languages. Her personality was surprisingly bland, though. I didn't know where her personality was or if it had the tiny hooks my Velcro personality needed.

After we'd reached her place, we started kissing. We were next to each other, with not much to say, in the little hallway by her kitchen, and she asked, "Do you want to take a shower?"—which should have been very arousing. Actually, I wanted to suggest we have a drink first, but I knew that James would consider this a mistake.

"All right," James said now. "She's sort of confused—" My phone rang and James reached over and answered it. He leaned back with the handset against his face. "Yeah, he's here," he said. He laughed and his eyes flitted to the ceiling. Covering the mouthpiece, he whispered, "It's not her."

"Who is it?" I whispered.

"Chuck," he whispered back.

"Give me that!"

"She hung up." And he put the handset back in the cradle.

"*She* hung up? That was her?"

She lived in an old church that had been turned into condos. The entryway was very nice—stone steps, stone walls. But once you were in her apartment, you couldn't tell the building used to be a church, though I knew we were hovering somewhere high in the nave, the space I always used to stare up at when I was a small person. I knew how much Joan was making and I knew it would be hard to pay to live that high up by herself. I thought of our age difference. Thirteen years. We were kissing there, in the former nave. And she wanted to shower, and then we did shower together.

"What are you doing answering my phone?" I asked James.

"She was calling for me," he said. "She just had to tell me something. She knew you wouldn't mind."

I furrowed my brow at him.

"I ran into her on my way over," he said, explaining.

"Did you tell her you'd made an important mistake?" The word was ***pharaoh***, misspelled *p-h-a-r-**o-a**-h,* in a piece of art, which made it harder to fix. It could have singlehandedly destroyed our credibility as a purveyor of educational materials for children.

He smiled faintly.

I wanted to tell him to leave, but that's what he wanted to do and I couldn't let him do what he wanted to do. I had to find out what it was he *didn't* want to do and then somehow get him to where he'd have to do it.

"I've let you become my friend," I said.

"You have?"

"But I can't have you messing with me. You still work for me. I cannot fathom why you would answer my phone—and not let me talk to her."

"Did you want to talk to her?"

In the shower with Joan, a lot of soaping went on between us. Sometimes her soaping was matter-of-fact, as if she were cleaning me, and other times it was not, as if we were having a sensual experience. "Relax," she said, but finally I couldn't stand it. I stepped out of the tub, dripping wet, still foamy in certain places. "Ray?" she said. Her voice was strained. "The way you were soaping me...," I mumbled. She laughed in an exasperated way. I stood at the sink and splashed water on myself to wash off the remaining suds, holding a towel to catch the water. Finally she stopped the shower and opened the curtain. She was fabulous. I thought maybe we could try again, without the soap. But she grabbed a towel and cinched it around herself and took another for her hair. She twisted a turban faster than I had ever seen one done. Maybe she felt rejected. Maybe she was starting to suspect that there was something "off" about me. She headed for her room, got me some clothes, including a pair of men's boxers, and let me dress in her living room while she dressed in her bedroom.

"You've got a lot of explaining to do," I told James.

He allowed a pained smile and scratched the back of his neck.

"I can fire you," I said.

"You can fire me," he said, singsong.

"All right, you're fired."

"Hey now, Ray. She wants to talk, but—"

"What makes you think you can torture me? Haven't I fired you? What're you doing here? Haven't I fired you?"

"I just wanted her to call because—" His eye started up again.

"You know, I don't care. You're making mistakes, and you're jerking me around."

"It was just going to be a joke. Honestly, Chief, you take things a little too—"

"I think you've been fired," I said, in a phony, nonchalant voice. The room was wavering. My head felt wrong. "Yes. Please leave now."

He got up, headed to the door. "You won't fire me," he said. "I'm a good proofreader." His eyelid was fluttering like a hummingbird. "You'll be up to your neck in mistakes."

"I like mistakes," I said.

"She respects you. She said that."

"But you can't see why."

"I'm a good proofreader, Chief."

But I knew he'd made mistakes.

"You don't want to fire me," he added quietly. "You need me."

"I do need you, but I'm firing you anyway. That's the kind of son of a bitch I am." I had no conviction behind this. I smiled. It was a fatuous smile, but I couldn't stop it. I saw what I was doing to his life, but then again I couldn't stop myself. I had to nail down this situation, somehow.

He pressed his mouth shut and left my office.

As soon as he was gone, I hesitated between calling her office number or her home number. She didn't have a cell phone; she said she didn't want one. It was almost six. If I called her office number, she might still be there and I would talk to her directly. Right then I thought it would be better to talk to her machine. So I called her home phone and told her machine: "Yes, always. And then some, you know it, and then some."

But she picked up.

"Is it you?" she said. "Wait, I just walked in the door. Is it you?"

"Not exactly," I said. I was so thrown off. *Had* James seen her before he came to my office? Had my phone even rung, or did James only suggest that to my memory by picking it up?

"What's up?" she said.

I could hear my nose-breathing, could hear it in my office, could hear it in the phone, could hear it in her ear, could hear it in the nave of the church.

"Ray?"

"Did you call my office a few minutes ago?"

"James wanted me to. He's so weird. He gave me his cell and told me to call him in your office—so you guys could hear the sound of me riding my bike home."

"You expect me to believe this?"

"Are you all right?"

"I'm afraid I'm going to have to find some way to fire you."

"Ray, please."

"It won't be easy for me."

"Listen, don't be so crazy. It was just James."

"Your pal," I said, very low.

"What?"

"Let's back up for a minute," I said. I raked my hair back from my forehead and held it taut with one hand, pulling toward the center of my head. "Why did you ever want to go out with me? I really need an answer to this."

"You seemed like a nice guy," she stammered. "We're not that serious. It was just to have some fun."

"Joan"—I had said her name—"Joan, we. . ." But because I was still at work in my glass office, I couldn't remind her we'd been naked together—and that she had soaped me. "I just want you to know that I haven't been able to show you the real me."

"I know, I know," she said, suddenly sounding very tired.

"Does that bother you?"

"It bothers me a lot, Ray. Listen, I know I probably shouldn't say this, but do you ever talk to somebody? I mean. . ."

"I talk to our friend James. And he talks to you. Isn't that enough talking?"

". . . I mean like a counselor? I've done it. It's—"

"I've always hired my own proofreaders," I said. "I'm not going to fire you. That would be low. You'd lose respect for me. You do respect me, don't you?"

"You can be a nice guy, you really can. Listen, let's just cool it for a while. Let's just maybe have lunch, maybe next week, and we can talk then. Or something."

I hung up on her.

Before I could congratulate myself for not firing her, I remembered years of perfumes, handbags, stockings hanging over the back of a wooden chair. I remembered aborted Christmas cards, botched hugs, petty criticisms I'd made, heavily redacted transcripts of horrific arguments, leaden conversations, and various groping clenches. I hated the idea that your character stays basically the same and that it follows you around your whole life.

I didn't want to be alone with these thoughts. I looked over the list of employees in my division, imagining their faces and what I had most recently said to each. Most of them I'd never tried to be friends with. I decided to write a brief memo to myself before I left the office. "Ray," I wrote, on a piece of company stationery, "try to be a little bit more friendly around the office." I knew I was sinking into something bad when I edited my note in proper proofreading style, making a careful caret and cross-out mark over "friendly," and then in the margin I wrote "congenial," for insertion, though I instantly knew it was not an improvement, so I put dots under "friendly" and crossed out "congenial" and wrote "stet" next to that, which meant leave it the way it was. I folded the paper once and put it in the top drawer of my desk, where there were other notes I had written to myself.

It was dark out now, the workday pretty much over, and through the air, across city blocks, other tall buildings stood at odd angles. I could see into them, and see other offices and cubicles, though not many people. In some elaborate office suite somewhere, hovering above the city, an executive was taking a private shower in a windowless bathroom. There was some comfort in this. Honestly, it was hard to leave my office at the end of the day. It seemed as if it wasn't actually possible to go.

I thought about Joan saying "Let's just cool it for a while" and basic hopefulness froze up in me. It was like when you're working on a computer and all of a sudden the cursor stops beating and you know the thing has crashed. I was thirty-eight years old. It seemed obvious that I would never establish a permanent loving relationship with a woman. I was frozen. I needed someone, someone I could trust, to help me leave the office, to help me get to my car.

For a second my head felt detached, like a balloon someone had just let go, and then a strong wave of dizziness hit. The corners of my mouth watered. I spread my hands on my glass desk and placed my forehead on the blotter. The desk soon seemed to be spinning. I slid out of my chair and lay down on my stomach and let my cheek rest on the carpet. I closed my eyes and that helped a little.

I told myself I wasn't that upset. The dizziness was just a state of mind; there was really nothing wrong with me. All I needed was a little compassion, to steady me. Maybe someone could find me facedown on the carpet, yet not be tempted to use that against me. Maybe an understanding person, a compassionate friend, could put a head in my office and say, "How's it hanging, Chief?" or, "Are you parked in the garage? I'm headed that way myself," as if lying on the floor was the same as slouching at your desk after a long day. Was that too much to ask? When had I forfeited the chance for a kind word from a friendly head?

I heard a vacuum cleaner in the distance. It seemed to be slowly working its way closer.

James, good proofreader, I thought, all is forgiven. I turned against myself and I hurt you. Come back, James. Come back! I will never fire you again.

Séance

The woman had moist. Damp pod inside. Intimate times, she was boiled snow pea slick. Months postmeeting, couldn't form a sentence. So directly affected by her, did I was. After we lost our baby, I sometimes went "yit" or "jit jit," my brain damp and _____ , while she absorbed the pain and gave off aseptic smiles. Current problem: I had raked the leaves into a pile. While she fumed, the leaves kept falling. Was I supposed to know piles of leaves aggravated her?

In the beginning we wanted heaven, pounding each other like felt piano hammers. Then we wanted her hair inserted into vases, dragged across legs, brilliantined, photographed. We wanted fresh blood in a deerskin pouch, hand cream in a rubber glove. We wanted commercially. Spinally. Greatly between the legs. In a desperate way.

"All right, all right, all right already!" (This was me perched on the peach basket, near the pile of leaves.) "For starters, you've bled me twelve different ways and mongered the plasma from traffic isles during morning rush hour. And another thing: I have a soul, all right, so don't go calling me a demon to all your friends. And another thing, I'm very strong. My hands are coordinated muscle fingers!"

"Oh, you're one to talk," she said. She unfurled her own fingers, slowly, over her stupid campfire.

"And another thing: Why a campfire in the middle of the goddamn suburbs when you've got every gadget known to man?"

"Huh," she said, sitting on a rock that bordered the empty garden. She raised fires there.

.   .   .

Our love had happened mightily, under the palm trees, Bora-Bora, designer swimsuits, honeymoon ribs that could kill. We detachable and brainless, undulating on the warm salty waves. Something like the pH of a womb. Talk. Crawl. In reverse order. She had faculties. She said she could grow a new version of us. She played up the magic of gestation. "I'm a shaman," she said. "Give me your liver."

"Oh, so now it's my liver." Ectomy.

Lengthwise we were fine. Alternatively, we fit. In bed, she would broach so many topics it was ridiculous. Do you think we could talk about the way your hair hangs? Do you think we could set aside a time to discuss the process by which seeds become plants? Have you ever wondered what it's like to be a mosquito? She broached so many topics, always a topic no one could be concerned with. Do you think egg whites would make a good shaving cream? What about egg yolks?

"Let me ask you something," she said one time, tracing figure eights on my chest with an unmanicured nail, "and don't take this the wrong way, but why are you always eating caramels?"

"Because they're the color of your ____ ."

She laughed because I couldn't say ____ . Too moist.

Some days it rained furiously, and when the sun finally came out, all I could think about was evaporation and the clouds to come. Her face decreased as each day went on until nightfall she was mainly a chin. I imagined the features north of her lips and loved her just the same. "You're so moist," I said one time.

"Don't lay that trip on me," she said, and she rolled away.

Her hair naturally formed nests, so she combed it an hour a day. Her hair gradually balled up, planetwise. Meanwhile, her topics unscrolled. She kept telling me things out of the blue, things that no one could ever conceive of saying and that could not be responded to in any way: "Balance your sleeves," "Make more noise when you enter a room," "Touch your own face less often." Believe me: it was a minute-to-minute struggle to be articulate in such a damp environment. Nevertheless, she became pregnant.

.   .   .

Our love was licit and, by the way, it became fractured and unholy. Sometimes when I think about the jobs we had at that time. How good they were and what lengths we went to jit to understand them, to perform our functions, even when she was starting to show. If an idea could break a man. I never said what I felt. Nothing I ever said sounded like how I yit.

My wife was a. Some things seemed to move just because we looked at them. Take that pile of leaves. That pile seemed to quiver when she made an issue out of it.

"What if something happens?" she said.

"It's just a pile of leaves."

The doctor said the fetus had gotten tangled in its own cord. There was nothing to.

.   .   .

Always so quick to solicit the spirits. In our neighborhood, séances were frowned upon, yet she was always organizing table tappings and ectoplasmic smackdowns. She claimed every mother is a medium for the spirit of her children because mothers are the portals of the spirit into this world. Our stillborn son, she said he was caught in the veil. She had to communicate with him. My plan was to help her.

"Why'd you have to rake that pile of leaves?" she started back in. "Why do you have to breathe so much air? It's like living with a bellows. Your hair seems misplanted on your head. Why don't you plow it under and sow something fresh? Why are you *always* putting on deodorant?"

Do not hesitate

"Why don't *you* get a wheelbarrow," I said, "and roll your sorrows to some field way the hell out there and just bury them? Why don't you just—"

to call your doctor

"Because you're always such a shit!" she concluded. Tears took off from her cheeks and floated in the air like dandelion seeds.

if you feel your baby's movements

. . .

Beneath the pilings. Her ocean sucked and withdrew. She ran the servants at her father's hacienda like so many cattle. After we lost, we took a trip there to ride her father's jittery Arabian horses and go sportfishing on his boat, *The Red Tree*. We almost drowned one day while we napped and a storm came up; we couldn't do shit against it. The storm

are not right.

blew over before we had put on our slickers. Then there was

the time we crystallized. She had a mood that we each completely understood. She said she felt as if she were dissolving and did I know exactly what the melting point of copper was. Why? "Because I've got some copper in me," she said, "and I think it has to get really hot to melt, so I think I'm all right. I'll never totally liquefy."

.   .   .

The sun slunk behind the hill. She kicked dirt over her fire, wiped her hands on her pants. Somebody once said that in between this moment and the next there is always a lapsing. There it was, lapsing on the grass.

"Moist," I murmured and thought *jit*. The gold leaves tumbled from the trees. The pile of leaves seemed to lift in a kind of inverted sympathy.

"Let me ask you something," she said. "Did you want the baby to die? Did you think it would ruin our marriage?"

Please don't.

"Yit," I mumbled.

"What did you say?"

"I thought the baby would bring us closer," I said. "A new version of us in one ____ ." But I couldn't say " ____ ," for some well-watered reason.

She saw only sarcasm, which meant things had come to an unholy end. I thought never to feel what. There was this sense, I think, as she went for the rake, that time-spent-together had been waiting with its breath sucked in, ready to release a whistling laugh. She picked up that rake and came after me. She chased me with the rake, around and around that pile of leaves, avoiding the pile like it was a bottomless well. I'd still be running if the three-year-old neighbor kid I had planted there in the pile—out of something desperate, stupid, misplanted, stupid, perverse (this being the anniversary of the fetus's death)—if the little kid hadn't popped his head out of the pile of leaves, spastic for clean breath.

"Sorry!" he gasped, for I had not yet given the signal for him to show himself. (I had forgotten the signal. Even now I have no idea what it.)

The next moment, we were all three on our backs, falling into the darkening sky.

Do not hesitate to call your doctor if you feel your baby's movements are not right.

My wife hasn't had a realization since. Much less sentence. She has a bazillion discrete bits of reality in her "in" box. She'll get to them, I guess. When we read the paper together, we struggle to establish the meaning of all the words. Maybe I've learned this much: never try to orchestrate someone else's cathartic séance. Maybe have I would and. I'd like to say she's become more dependent on me, but she's always signaling, I can do it, I can do it. And this with a rake in her hand. Ready to scatter me if I lay my hand to something.

A Talented Individual

When had it dawned on him that he was a talented individual? Was it on the first day of second grade when Sister Rose asked him if he wanted yet another sheet of math problems while other kids struggled with their first? Was it the eighth-grade forensics tournament in which he placed first in extemporaneous speaking? Or was it his MBA in marketing from the Kellogg School at Northwestern, a top-five B-school?

It seemed to Ben Brown as if he had always known.

On top of this, his wife, Paula, was smart and physically fit. He met her when she was halfway through the sociology PhD program at NU. They graduated the same brilliant June day, took a stroll on the lakefill, and gazed longingly to the south where the distant towers of Chicago stood hazy against the blue sky. He took her hand, squeezed it, then brought it to his lips. "There it is," he said, feeling as if he'd already made it.

The idea was to follow their dreams together, with neither career taking precedence. As it turned out, the academic job market was brutal, and Paula was lucky to snag a tenure-track gig at Western Michigan University. It meant a move to Kalamazoo, which, coincidently, was just down 131 from her family in Grand Rapids. What did he think of that? Well, there was a Fortune 500 medical appliance company with its world headquarters in Kalamazoo—that's what he thought of that! It wasn't, "Hey, kids, come see Dad's commercial on TV," but it paid well, and selling to doctors and hospitals meant he wouldn't need to hide his intelligence under a bushel.

Within five years, he rose to marketing director for the Surgical Power Tool segment of the Instruments Division, selling the Life-Force line of handheld drills and precision-tipped reciprocal saws for cutting through ribs and boring holes in skulls and reaming out hip sockets. These were handsome machines, yes? And who wouldn't pay to minimize soft-tissue damage? He'd traveled to a dozen countries, talking to doctors, listening aggressively, demoing devices that enhanced thousands of lives. He'd leveraged his people skills to coach up his subordinates and drive an effective team. His work had all the trappings of a meaningful vocation.

By his midthirties, VP for marketing of the entire Instruments Division was in his sights, and he was looking higher. But then a faux pas here, an ill-advised argument there, a presentation he inexplicably fumbled, and he was hit with his first big professional disappointment: passed over for a promotion. Could it be that not everyone saw him as he saw himself?

.   .   .

"You're still moping, goddamn it," Paula said, seven months later, as they scuffed along the beach path to her family's ancestral cottage on Crystal Lake. "Figure out a new goal." She was a shrewd analyst of the structural causes of rural poverty and knew what was worth whining about. It shamed him that he needed picking up at all. He didn't want to be *that* guy. The people he read about in magazine profiles never needed bracing slaps from their life partners—they were arrogant bastards floating on clouds of success.

The family was on a back-to-basics vacation, northern Michigan. Beijing and the Great Wall were postponed for lack of funds. He'd gotten ahead of himself, thinking with promotion dollars that were not forthcoming. At the beach, on the daily outing for ice cream, he took a good look at his offspring, wondering if he could reconnect after weeks of sales trips. Six-year-old Nathan was bowlegged. When did that happen? He'd gotten a buzz haircut. Whose idea? Daughter Skyler wore tight lingerie-style tops with eye shadow and thong underwear (he'd seen it on the laundry table!), and she was, what—eleven? Eye shadow on a beach vacation? He needed to keep them in line and on track.

After two days of rain, the clouds finally blew apart, and he decided it was time to grill. Fresh whitefish for Paula with a special sauce, hot dogs for the kids, a red-hearted burger for himself. The kids scarfed their dogs in less than a minute, bolted their lemonade as if competing in a drinking game, and asked to be excused, a fistful of potato chips each for the road.

Their abrupt departure opened a trapdoor into a howling, sucking loneliness, like a hole in the bottom of an airplane at night.

"Sit down and stay awhile!" he shouted after them.

Skyler scrunched her shoulders as if she'd been whipped. Nathan ran off down the two-track driveway, pursued by a bear.

"Jesus, Ben," Paula said. "Did you hear yourself?"

"No, I can't fucking hear myself," he snapped. "I've got fake ears screwed into my head!"

He felt like a total ass. In his review before the lost promotion, his boss had suggested Ben had an "irritable streak." True, he sometimes got impatient, but that was because he was bent on getting things done. Didn't people want things done? Now the wind lifted a paper plate and he swatted it down. He stuffed it into a plastic trash bag he'd hung from a nail on the picnic table. He'd rigged that up himself. Always innovating.

Paula's warning look turned from angry to concerned. She was usually three steps ahead of his self-awareness, and he was grateful she didn't always use that position to crush him.

"I'm sorry, Paula," he muttered.

"It's a vacation," she said, mustering some cheerfulness. "Remember?"

It seemed that his apology surrounded the situation yet somehow left his fault exposed, the way surgeons cover a patient's body except for where they're operating.

.   .   .

So how could he refuse when Paula suggested a night at the Benzie County Fair?

He wanted to be excited. He remembered some awesome times as a kid at Dandelion Park. Midways used to give him a dreamy sense of possibility, as if you really could get lost in the fun house, as if the Alpine Express really did speed through the mountains as opposed to rumbling around a rickety oval.

They parked in the grass, skirted some squishy puddles, paid up. There were hours of pitiless August sunlight left. You couldn't win at this time of year: either it was dreary when it rained or the sun came out with such force all you wanted to do was take cover. Just past the gate, vendors sold homemade jewelry, 4-H exhibits touted rabbit agility and fun facts about sheep, and a stage still shimmered with tinsel bunting where the Queen of the Fair had apparently been crowned. There were stalls with sheep and cows and hogs and one llama. A sign noted that a sixty-pound piglet had become a three-hundred-pound sow. What kind of accomplishment was that—put the thing in a pen, feed it a shitload, and make it fat? Here you go—a blue ribbon!

Paula, of course, struck up in-depth conversations with the barn people, working her way into questions about the local farm co-op. He half admired her strategy: bring this bumblefuck world toward your mind in a certain way, and all of a sudden everyone was important and you didn't have to feel depressed.

The rides were more violent than he remembered—light-rimmed contraptions shaped like drilling derricks, pendulums, corkscrews. The games, however, were the same cheesy classics—Alley Ball, Duck Hunt, Hoops, Day at the Races. They turned the kids loose with a wad of tickets.

"Hey, doll," he said to Paula, "I'm going to win you something." He pointed to a row of plush rabbits hung from a rope by their chins. The basketballs weren't regulation, the rims slightly warped. He played three times but failed to make a shot.

"That's all right," Paula said. She laughed lightly. One of her brothers had played wide receiver at Michigan.

Ben said nothing. He couldn't afford to lose his temper again. Things were getting worse. There'd been the high-fructose corn syrup rant he'd delivered a few months ago to the terrified waitress at Denny's when she'd served the kids their chocolate chip pancakes covered with an obscene mountain of whipped cream from a can (the squiggle marks gave it away). Then Skyler didn't lock up her bike at the Y, it got stolen, and he went off on her. "Bikes don't grow on trees!" he'd yelled moronically. Skyler had burst into tears, and he'd ended up apologizing. The other day at work, he'd blurted, "You know what, I don't give a crap about *the journey*. Let's just hit our numbers and have a drink!" An embarrassed silence had followed. Sometimes he felt at odds with everyone he talked to.

They walked through the grounds on a crowded asphalt path. Occasionally, they caught sight of their children slamming into each other in the bumper cars or shrieking in a hammer-shaped pendulum that swung back and forth until it turned beyond 360 degrees. When they got off the Tilt-a-Whirl, Skyler took her brother's hand until they were clear of the ride. Paula wordlessly squeezed Ben's arm, as if to say, "Isn't it better when we all get along?"

"Nice night," he said into the air, doing his best to respond in kind.

At the far end of the midway, they came upon a tightrope strung between two platforms about fifteen feet off the ground. A small red bicycle with tireless wheel rims was hooked onto a railing on the left platform.

Did this fair really have a high-wire act? A cardboard clock said the next performance would be at 9:00 P.M.

"Hey, let's stick around for the show," he said. "I want to see that." The prospect of a legitimate circus act boosted his spirits.

"Sure, why not," Paula said.

But it was only seven thirty. He couldn't stomach the rides, so they'd be wandering the midway, talking if they could, until nine.

"You want an ice cream?" he asked Paula.

There was a little ice-cream trailer nearby. *Old-Fashioned Root Beer Floats* was emblazoned across the front in purple-and-yellow script. They got in line behind a heavy woman ordering a sundae. A squealing toddler squirmed in a stroller next to her. "Shush!" the woman said. "I told you!"

Inside the trailer was an elderly woman with obviously dyed curly blonde hair, canal-deep wrinkles, and a chin that gave her a mannish look. She bent over a cooler with an ice-cream scoop, working slowly.

The toddler screamed and mushed his hands into his own

face, as if the expression required to show his pain could only be achieved manually.

"I told you!" his mother said. "Shut it!"

Ben had a secret sympathy for people who got upset in public. It was a horrible world sometimes. He knew Paula wouldn't say anything, but he felt implicated in the mother's behavior. Finally, the woman bent down and unfastened the toddler, picked him up, and slung him spread-eagled against her hip. He quieted some.

At last, the ice-cream lady foamed out a gurgling snake of whipped cream, put a maraschino cherry on top, and pushed the sundae cup through the window. The memory of his Denny's whipped cream rant made Ben's face flush. The customer said, "Thank you!" and walked away, holding the child against her hip with one arm. With her other hand she managed to hold the sundae and push the empty stroller by two fingers on one handle.

Paula ordered a root beer float, Ben an M&M flurry. The old woman began scooping hard yellow ice cream, activating vestigial arm muscles within the sag of leathery, pleated skin. She was obviously too poor to retire.

"That was me at dinner tonight, wasn't it?" he asked Paula.

"What do you mean?"

"Having a meltdown."

Paula sighed. "What do you want me to say, Ben?"

"You don't have to say anything."

"You're maneuvering me. I don't like it."

"I've got to say stuff sometimes."

"And I'm supposed to call you out, so I'll be in the wrong?"

He decided to let it drop. She was getting worked up.

A younger but dissipated-looking man entered the cramped trailer with a twenty-pound bag of ice on his shoulder, silver-rimmed glasses askew. He had greasy salt-and-pepper hair parted to one side, and he wore a filthy blue-gray T-shirt. He laid the bag of ice into the cooler and pulled the sliding hatch shut.

"Anything else?" he asked the old woman.

"No," she said, and he left the trailer.

The man walked off down the asphalt path in a slanted, staggering way, as if on a listing ship.

"You're just finding some way to beat yourself up," Paula restarted in a tense, low voice, "and then I'm supposed to do something about it."

She gathered her dark hair, lifted if off her neck, and wound it against the back of her head. Her bare neck used to turn him on, but now it just housed vocal cords.

The ice-cream lady took a two liter of root beer from the refrigerator. She twisted off the cap with no fizzing sound. She topped off the float, handed it to Paula, and started in on the flurry. She slid open the cooler again and scooped ice cream into a tall metal cup—five times with the same unhurried, precise motion.

Ben found the pace maddening. She poured in milk, attached the cup to a blender, and ran it for a good minute. Then she fished out an unopened bag of M&Ms. More customers were waiting, but instead of quickly ripping open the bag, she reached into a drawer and pulled out a scissors. She clipped open the bag, poured some into a small measuring cup, shook about three-quarters of them into the flurry, and stirred them in.

"Whipped cream?" she asked in a smoker's voice.

Startled, he said, "No."

Even as he worried that the high-fructose corn syrup lobby was trying to make his kids diabetic, he had become an ice-cream addict—at least it had real dairy—and he knew it showed. Maybe his weight gain had been costing him image-wise at work, but he knew his lean, hypercompetent self still lived inside his swelling body.

The ice-cream lady poured the rest of the mixture into the cup, sprinkled on the remaining M&Ms and handed the flurry to Ben. "OK, let's see," she said, looking at the counter.

Ben had already calculated, but he didn't say anything.

"I'm not very good at math," she said.

He focused on a dusty stuffed monkey sitting on a shelf by a sleeve of cups.

"Six dollars," she said.

"Well, you got it right!" he said, handing over the cash. That sounded condescending, so he hurriedly crammed a five-dollar bill into her tip jar.

They took seats on a bench facing the tightrope. The sun was going down and it angled into their faces.

He didn't want to talk about how depressed he was feeling, but he had no other topic with Paula.

For some reason, the tightrope reminded him of his book project. A few years ago, a friend from college had written a book for business travelers about how to stay connected to your children when you were on the road. It was an appealing and flimsy book filled with lists, games, and contrived phone call scripts that had somehow gotten his friend on *Good Morning America*. Who knew about traveling and being disconnected from your kids better than Ben did? The success of his friend felt like having his sternum split with the ultra-lightweight LifeForce 1200 handheld reciprocal saw and then drawn open with a LifeForce S series rib spreader—just so he could eat his heart out.

In the wake of his lost promotion, he'd come up with an idea no one could scoop—a series of children's books about difficult surgeries a friend or relative might face: *Grandma's Getting a New Hip!*, *What's So Funny about Open Heart Surgery?*, *Trouble in My Uncle's Brain*. Paula had said the early drafts put too much emphasis on the power tools used in the operations. That was three months ago. He'd been meaning to get back to the project ever since.

"Everything's still in front of you," a tiny voice in his head said now. Yes, it is, he answered. He perked up slightly.

"How's your float?" he asked Paula.

"Eh," she said.

His flurry was horrible. The M&Ms had turned hard as freezer-burned pebbles. As they slid and cracked against his molars, he feared his teeth would break.

"How's your research coming?" he asked.

She was working on a book of her own, *Socializing Success*, which would prove that the best predictor of academic achievement was a peer group of at least three students with similar goals.

There were enormous policy implications.

"I can't decide how many years of data I'll need," she said.

She said many more things as the sun went down. He thought she might dedicate her book to him because he had made himself listen so well, and just after he thought this, they sat in silence. The cardboard clock stared back at them.

Ben checked his iPhone: 8:03.

"Let's see what the kids are up to," he said.

They found their children and wordlessly followed them from ride to ride.

They stood on the pavement and looked up as Nathan and Skyler were spun flat in an enormous centrifuge. As the ride wound down, he heard himself say, "I might get back to my children's book idea."

"What brought this on?" Paula asked.

"Nothing in particular."

"I'm sorry, I shouldn't have put it that way."

"I thought you wanted me to have new goals."

"I do. I want you to have realistic goals."

"Realistic," he said flatly, trying to keep calm.

The kids had disembarked from the centrifuge and walked toward them.

"Oh man!" Skyler said woozily. Nathan smiled dreamily, as if on drugs.

"I want a treat," Nathan said.

Ben couldn't say no because he'd just had ice cream, so he sent them to the old lady's trailer, while he and Paula found the same seats in front of the tightrope.

A few more people were waiting for the show. A string of lights running above the tightrope had been turned on. Floodlights brightened the area.

"Look," Paula said softly. "I think you're very depressed. I think you need help."

"I don't think so," he said.

"Then I need help. I don't like it when you get like this. It's hard on both of us."

"How am I like anything?" he asked angrily.

Skyler came back with Nathan and said the ice-cream trailer was closed. Paula got up and said she'd help the kids find something.

How dare she say he was depressed! Sure, he'd thought it himself, but now that it was in her head, he couldn't get at it and change it, so it threatened to become an objective reality. No doubt his psyche had a leak somewhere; he'd had inklings of this. Talented people often bore extraordinary psychological burdens that indirectly fueled achievement. Maybe his impatience had been driven all along by a sense that everything could slip away. But she made him sound like a basket case.

A few minutes later, a woman in a sequined gold leotard walked from behind the ice-cream trailer toward a tall white pole that stood in a grassy area beyond the tightrope setup. Ben hadn't even really noticed the pole before, half thinking it was some kind of antenna. It was at least a hundred feet tall and staked with guy wires. The woman's body had an odd, Photoshopped quality to it: she had the toned legs of a twenty-year-old, an almost barrel-like torso, long arms, and a head with stiff curly hair too large for the whole ensemble, yet she walked steadily. When he caught a better look at her face, he murmured into the air: "Is that the woman from the ice-cream stand?"

The woman in the sequined outfit reached the pole and began climbing up, lifting her knees quite high to reach each foothold. There was no net, no harness. She slowly rose above the reach of the floodlights, a vaguely luminous shape. The sun had gone all the way down.

Paula and the kids came back carrying elephant ears on paper plates.

"My God," Ben said to Paula as they sat down, "it's the ice-cream lady climbing that pole behind the high wire!"

"I wondered about her," Paula said coolly. "She had a red blouse on. All the other vendors are in green polos."

Ben had completely missed this.

Then a man in a brown-and-yellow tuxedo with sequins on the lapels approached a microphone standing nearby in the grass. Every strand of salt-and-pepper hair was combed into place. His glasses glinted in the lights. It was the guy who brought the ice!

"Ladies and gentlemen, and children of all ages!" he said. "Let me direct your attention to the daring performer climbing the sway pole behind me." A spotlight picked up the woman who was now almost two-thirds of the way up the pole. "A little later in the show, she will perform amazing aerial feats—Marla Fassanari!"

Marla stopped climbing and sat herself on what must have

been a tiny ledge that Ben couldn't even see. She waved to the crowd. Her name rang a bell. The Fearless Fassinaris were a famous circus family. He had a vague memory of seeing them on TV when he was a kid. What was she doing at this pathetic county fair?

Inane upbeat music began playing through a pair of loud-speakers. When Ben returned his gaze to ground level, the tuxedoed man had removed his jacket, revealing a yellow shirt with a ruffled front. With a step-and-slide motion, carrying a long floppy pole across his waist, he began walking in ballet shoes up one of the guy wires that tethered the left platform of the tightrope. He reached the platform and walked across the wire. Safe on the other side, he raised his right hand with a flourish.

Ben applauded vigorously. He looked around. There were maybe thirty people watching. About half of them clapped.

The man performed some jumps and turns on the wire. Then he rode his small red bicycle across the wire forward and backward. He hooked his bike on the right platform and carried out a white chair with two bars connecting the front legs to the back legs. After situating the chair under himself on the wire, he sat on it. Then he sat on top of the chair's narrow back with his feet on the seat, always careful, never really having to correct his balance. The crowd obliged with applause as the man stood up on the chair, and people really gave it up for him when he did a handstand on the seat. Then he slowly dismounted and carried the chair off the wire. He was done. He was safe, shrugging back into his tuxedo jacket.

The spotlight again flashed on Marla, way up on the sway pole. She was standing, one hand holding the pole, her other hand flung up into the air.

"I Will Survive" began blasting over the speakers:

"At first I was afraid . . . I was petrified . . ."

"And now, ladies and gentlemen," the tuxedo man said, "allow me to introduce to you one of the greatest aerial acrobats the world has ever known, the marvelous Marla Fasssss—anari!" Marla saluted and started climbing even higher on the pole while the music throbbed. "A member of the famous Fearless Fassanaris, she performed in her first circus at the age of three. When she was twenty-eight, her dear aunt died on this very apparatus. A year later, Marla attempted the sway pole for the first time and has been performing on it for *forty-five years*, a Guinness World Record!"

Ten feet from the top of the pole, Marla started to lean back and forth, causing the pole to sway.

"I can't believe she's doing this," Ben said. "This is so crazy!"

She let go with one hand and one foot, and he felt he had to catch himself from pitching down a tall flight of stairs.

As a kid, watching circus performers and motorcycle jumpers and swimmers with sharks on TV, he had comforted himself with the idea that they wouldn't broadcast it if something truly terrible was going to happen. But anything could happen now.

Abruptly, she slipped her wrist into a strap and swung the rest of her body away from the pole, holding on to the strap with just one hand. She raised one knee high and pointed her feet, her left hand outstretched, as if reaching to take a glass of wine off a table.

"Ladies and gentlemen, she's a seventy-three-year-old *great-grandmother*, performing the most spectacular aerial feats just for you!"

Ben clapped furiously. He was afraid of heights, his stomach clenched painfully on roller coasters, yet his imagination took him up to Marla. He felt the wind blowing in his hair, the horizon tossing from side to side as the pole swayed. Staying alive depended on hands and feet, and they were blind appendages that could only be controlled through mental commands that suddenly seemed mysterious and unreliable.

"I Will Survive" kept blasting. The singer confessed to oh so many nights feeling sorry for herself, but now she held her head up high. Marla slipped a foot into the strap and hung upside down by one ankle.

He had to look away. He put his elbows on his knees and his face in his hands. Why was she risking her life for thirty people? She wasn't famous anymore. It was so pointless! He stared at his toenails poking out of his sandals. Fourteen-hour days in dress shoes had proved conducive to a yellow fungus. It was perverse how lately the more time he spent on the job the less he seemed to get done. He listened for the screams that would signify she was falling. Her body would thud against the rain-softened ground. He would sense the impact in his hideous toes. No surgery could repair what would be left of her.

When he looked up again, both of her feet were stuck to the pole somehow and she was essentially standing sideways, her arms outstretched, projecting like a human flag. The pole was still swaying. "I Will Survive" wouldn't stop. Marla did an amazing midair sit-up, gripped the pole, unhooked her foot, and began climbing higher, all the way to the top of the pole, where a triangular bracket jutted horizontally into the air.

She sat in the bracket and kicked up her pointed toes, like a burlesque dancer sitting in an enormous martini glass. She climbed out of the bracket, onto her knees. Then she hooked her legs back into the bracket, facing down. She seemed a little tired, a little clumsy, arcing her torso over the void, extending her baggy-skinned arms into the air.

"I Will Survive" ended, and Ben unclenched his fists. All she had to do was climb down.

"Ladies and gentlemen, I want you to know that on top of that pole is a great-grandmother, seventy-three years young! Marla

Fassss—anari!!" The announcer raised both arms in the air, bunching the shoulders of his tuxedo jacket around his ears.

The crowd applauded more loudly now, though Ben couldn't tell whether they were more appreciative of Marla for being a great-grandmother or for performing this wildly dangerous stunt instead of sleeping in front of the TV with a bowl of Chex Mix in her lap.

"Oh, please come down," he said out loud. He felt Paula glance at him.

New music kicked in. It sounded like an up-tempo Muzak version of the *2001* theme, heavy on the drum machine.

"And now," the tuxedo man said, "the marvelous Marla Fassanari will perform her final feat of aerial magic!" Ben forced out a puff of air. Madness! Unrelenting madness! "One hundred and ten feet above solid ground, without a net, without a safety cord, she will free stand on top of the pole. Ladies and gentlemen, please offer Marla your prayers and your undivided attention!"

The music pounded away, egging on the unfolding disaster. Ben felt himself sagging, like a balloon squeezed so hard and so steadily that it leaks air without popping. Something essential was being wrung out of him—maybe his will itself.

Marla clambered to her knees. The pole was still swaying slightly but she proceeded. She got her feet under her.

"Cautiously," the announcer said in a hushed voice. "Cautiously. The wind's a little frisky up there . . ."

Ben thought the world was unbelievably horrible.

Marla put up her hands, palms facing forward, and slowly stood up.

"Cautiously balancing . . . at the edge of eeee—ternity . . ."

Her hands paddled in the air, tweaking her balance, saving her life. She kept her knees bent and lifted her hands over her head, more like she was under arrest than triumphantly saluting.

"And there she is, just for you—Marla Fassanari!!"

The crowd applauded heartily, though they clapped no more intensely than the audience had at Skyler's appalling year-end band concert. That was all he could take. She must start down immediately.

"And now, in the ultimate test of skill and daring," the announcer intoned in a deeper voice, "Marla attempts to *sway the pole* from her precarious perch!"

A sense of nightmare bled in from the edges of Ben's vision.

Marla slowly pumped her knees from side to side, and the pole began to sway again. She held her hands out to the side, her knees bent like a surfer. With each pass she swayed a little farther, a little faster, in each direction. Her posture was crouched, not confident, almost shaky. Another inch of sway and she would tip over and plunge.

"Jesus H. Christ," Ben heard himself say. "Get the fuck down! I can't take it—it's so fucking stupid!"

He realized he had shouted. For an instant he thought Marla had heard him and he'd broken her concentration and she was going to fall. He looked down, bracing himself for the hysterical screams, the pulverizing thud, but apparently she wasn't falling. He felt Paula and Skyler and Nathan staring at him. Everyone was looking at him. His friend's book didn't have a chapter on freaking out in front of your children. Paula would pick her moment, probably when they were back in Kalamazoo, and hand him a slip of paper with a name and a phone number of a therapist on it. She might even stand there until he dialed.

When he looked up again, Marla was still standing on high, her arms tentatively raised, the sway pole moving ten feet in each direction, swishing in the wind, her knees now adjusting surprisingly little. Insane old woman! She had carefully clipped open the bag of M&Ms. She had asked him if he wanted whipped cream. He had stood ready to correct her math. He had pitied her. Forty-five years on the sway pole without missing a step, forty-five years without losing it. The very things that bothered him about her were her strengths. She wasn't slow—she was methodical. She was subtle and dogged, careful and bold, oblivious yet focused. She could stand the suspense when outcomes were uncertain. He suspected that these qualities constituted all there was to her talent. Or maybe they were just what kept her talent from killing her.

The announcer triumphantly called out Marla's name. The audience gave her their best applause. Most who were sitting stood up and clapped.

He stood and applauded as well, but then he turned his back on Marla and faced the midway. The Pirate Ship lurched up and back. The painted horses on the bright Merry-Go-Round rose and fell. He suddenly had an uncanny vision of what he looked like from behind: his thick neck thrust forward like a horse pulling a wagon, his doughy back swelling in his navy polo shirt, his bald spot like a circle shaved for a brain surgeon. He'd long ago stopped being talented in any meaningful way. On the Atomic Drop, people were strapped to a sort of wall-less elevator; they rose to the top of the shaft while lights chased upward. Then the machine dropped them and they all screamed.

Helmet of Ice

It was a cold November day, and our dry boats rested one hundred yards from a sea broken into churning black heaves of water between jostling bergs. I feared my father would chase me with his ax, as a joke, forcing me to run over the hard creases of shore ice, which were sharp enough to cut through my sealskin pants and gash my legs. My mother lay on her stomach among the women. For some reason she was acting as if she were a seal pup—her cough could sometimes be heard above the wind that was dying as the clouded sun fell toward the horizon.

My father's harassment had become intolerable. This morning he had scoffed when I spilled whale oil while pouring some into a smaller container that my mother wanted to give to a destitute neighbor. So I had taken his rifle and set it in a snowbank a mile from the village and baited it with the head of a seal. Then I'd built a cowl over the seal head with a piece of tarp and old tent poles. I had seen a polar bear hunting the ice edge near there and hoped it would nose under the cowl, take the bait, and trigger my father's rifle.

"Have you seen my gun?" my father had asked me around noon.

"No," I said.

I had been listening all day for the rifle's report. I wanted to slip away and inspect my trap in case I had missed the sound. If the bear had been shot, I would reveal everything to my father. I would share the meat and earn respect and my father would never harass me again.

Now my father was talking among the men, near our dry boats, leaning on the handle of his ax. All the men wore caribou-hide parkas trimmed with fox fur. I would walk by slowly and continue to my rifle set. My step was light, no louder than grains of sugar stirred in a metal canister.

As I was passing the men, I overheard my father loudly giving advice: "Arch your back while screaming and your sound will carry another mile." The men nodded carefully. "Grab yourself by the neck first thing every morning, and let that be the last time you are caught off guard each day!"

Then I heard the faint report of a gun. I almost ran, but I stopped altogether and lifted my nose toward the distant sound. My father squinted at me.

One of the men thumped his mittens together to beat away the cold. My father turned back to the men: "Do all sons hate all fathers?" he asked. "I have always thought so, and this is why I must sit quietly for days at a time." Every eye avoided every other eye. "Do you fathers have any hobbies?" he continued. "My favorite is to lie still with a helmet of ice on my head. I find this helps me to master difficult thoughts and feelings."

It was getting harder and harder to stand this harassment. I would run to my trap, though it might set off his pursuit instinct. I would see the bullet in the bear's forehead, then reveal all. I would go. But I felt him looking, and I couldn't go. For what if the bear was still alive?

Quality Snacks

Assembled there in a fifth-floor conference room at the North American headquarters in Plano were twelve of Frito-Lay's finest minds. No, we weren't the very top of the org chart—though Helen was VP for Consumer Strategy, Insights, and Growth—but we represented a crucial creative force. I believed a company was driven by its products. Period. As a senior project scientist for the Doritos platform, I had devoted my entire professional career to creating quality snacks.

I had also been falling in love with Helen for about a year, ever since she joined us after a divorce followed by a management shakeout at Procter & Gamble. Her meeting style was as crisp as her business suits. She sported the short hair and large lapels of a Carly Fiorina, HP's ceiling-busting ex-CEO, though I thought she was ten times as attractive, with balls of steel.

She called the meeting to order and asked for reports on Nacho Cheesier, Guacamole, and Four Cheese. Nacho was doing fine, but after Cynthia from Accounting did units of 4C and Guac by region, there was a sort of sad silence in the room. Nacho Cheesier, of course, was simply a new and improved version of our flagship product, but where was new growth going to come from to meet the aggressive targets of Nancy Sargent, president of Frito-Lay North America?

"Thank you, Cynthia," Helen finally said. Then her eyes took in the rest of us. "People, that's what's in the rearview mirror. Call it roadkill, call it a good effort, I don't really care. The question is, where are we headed?"

Eyes lost themselves in the polished oak table. Someone had done a marvelous wax job; it was like looking into a clear shallow pond.

"I say we fire the bastards on the Guac and 4C teams," I tossed in.

This prompted spotty laughter, some of it nervous, especially from two of the newbie engineers who were clearly unsettled by the failure of their first major product launches. Without my track record—I cut my buds on Taco, which in my mind will always be our flagship flavor—they couldn't afford the joke like I could.

"No, seriously," I said. "Let me throw some corn paste at the wall and see what sticks."

My impressive title aside, I was essentially a baker, and at a less enlightened company, I would have already been put in my place: Leave the big strategic decisions to us, Reggie. But on our product development team, there were only ideas, not the people who spoke them.

"If we want," I continued, "we can say the angle was right, the flavoring was wrong, for which I take full responsibility, but I think we're finding that we've pretty much exhausted all the readily exploitable Tex-Mex *flavors*. We can keep going down that road, to massage Helen's metaphor,"—I turned beet red after I said this—"and maybe we'll hit the jackpot with a chili and lime or something like that, but I think we've got to make a leap."

There was a deep sigh from Janice Howard, our ombudsperson for cultural sensitivity. She'd been hired in the midseventies, not long after the company finally capitulated in the controversy over the Frito Bandito, and was credited with thereafter keeping FL's nose clean of any gender or race discrimination catastrophes. She operated in some amorphous management area between Legal and Human Resources, and always seemed to committee above and beyond her rank. Though she wasn't an obvious candidate, she'd applied for the position Helen landed. Perhaps Janice was being kept in the loop to appease her—word was that she was considering a weight discrimination suit against the company. Janice, known to be a not infrequent consumer of FL products, was pushing three hundred pounds, while Helen, a few inches taller at about five-eight, couldn't have been more than one-forty.

"I don't know if we can afford another one of your leaps, Reggie," Janice said. I didn't know exactly what she meant by this, but if she was implying that either 4C or Guac had been my idea, she was dead wrong. With those decisions, like a good soldier, like a man in charge of turning a flavoring idea into a reality that could be sprayed on actual triangular chips, I had just said: "We'll do our best." And we had. Sure, maybe 4C ended up "a cacophony rather than a blend," as one consumer who called the 800 number put it, and maybe there was a slight mealiness to the avocado taste in Guac. Honestly, I wasn't a huge fan of either one myself. But this wasn't "Reggie's Own"; this was Frito-Lay, and we had taste-tested those flavors to death and tweaked the recipes until we were recalculating everything from maltodextrin to Monterey Jack, making samples until our eyeballs bled. Anyway, this wasn't the first time Janice had made insinuations tarring me with the failure of those products, but I thought it would be disloyal to the development team to argue with her.

So I pressed on, as upbeat as possible: "What if we could get people to stop thinking of us as a snack chip and instead start thinking of us as *the main course*? Isn't that the holy grail in this business? I think Taco flavor is a good example."

Janice rolled her eyes in a manner that conveyed, "Here he goes with Taco again."

"A taco is actually a meal, not a flavor," I persevered. "It's a meal that happens to have a particular taste that everyone loves. This would be incredibly tricky and could cause a hoopla with some of the consumer groups, but what if we developed meal flavors like Burrito and Chicken Quesadilla and Enchilada, or even Refried Beans? And what if we put into the mix some of the vitamins and minerals you could expect to get from those foods? You know, vitamin-fortified Doritos with meal flavors. You put three or four different Doritos on your plate, and you have sort of a Mexican dinner right there."

"Well, isn't that kind of what we did with Guacamole?" said Hector, one of the young engineers.

"Are you taking Reggie seriously?" Janice asked him, and she shook her head ruefully. "I'm sorry, but it would be a disaster. Consumer groups would indeed see the hypocrisy in a second."

My eye went from Helen to Dick Behuniak in Marketing. It seemed to me that his best work to date had been promoting himself to Helen. Helen herself sat with her hands lightly on the armrests of her chair; she was swiveling almost imperceptibly. Dick had a foot crossed on his knee and his legal pad braced against his bent leg; he seemed to be taking notes. I couldn't read his face, but he finally looked up at me.

"It's interesting, Reggie," he said. "It really is. Could be a tough sell, though."

"But it wouldn't be hypocritical," I said defensively. "The vitamins would actually be in there. I mean, we could even shelve them where you get your black beans and your taco shells and your enchilada kits. The tagline could be, 'Let's just have Doritos.' You've got this working mom—or dad!—in a dither: meetings and phone calls all day, then it's six o'clock, a busting headache, the kids are screaming, now come up with dinner! Then it hits: 'Let's just have Doritos!' Commercial ends with the family around the table, shaking chips onto their plates from like four different bags—"

"Sounds like *Soylent Green*," Cynthia threw in, referencing the highly nutritious sci-fi cracker that unfortunately turns out to be made from people. Everyone but me belly-laughed. I tried to take this as a tribute to our organization: even one of our numbers jocks could get off a good one-liner. Actually, I didn't mind the interruption. My voice had been rising in volume. My ears felt as red as a coil on an electric stove.

.   .   .

After the meeting, I found Mike Wardell from Purchasing walking alongside me on the way to the elevators.

"You need to get out more," he said. Mike had recently given up on his hair recovery efforts and shaved himself bald, which gave him a severe but hip look. We stopped short of the elevators, in front of a small framed print of a Rivera mural. The sunshine through a narrow window made a parallelogram of light on the carpet.

"That bad?" I said, unable to make eye contact.

"Reggie, that just wasn't you in there."

"I know, but—"

"I'm worried."

I finally looked up from the sunshine and caught Mike's stern gray-blue eyes. I had a full head of hair.

"One more thing," he said, "assuming you're really listening: if you've got a crush on Helen, ask her out, don't showboat at a meeting."

I was speechless, absolutely found out.

Mike clapped a hand on my shoulder. "You're forty-nine years old, Reggie," he said, lowering his voice. "The door is closing."

A red digital "5" lit above one of the elevators. There was a ding and the doors eased apart.

.   .   .

Monosodium glutamate, arguably the "active ingredient" in Doritos, has gotten a bad rap in some quarters. MSG creates a pleasing beefy sensation in the taste buds and increases dopamine release into the *nucleus accumbens*, the reward center of the brain—the same region, incidentally, that's activated during sex and drug use and which many scientists consider the "site" of addiction. No wonder even terrible dictators like Saddam Hussein were powerless against Doritos. In fact, there were dark years after my own divorce, before Helen's arrival, when some apparently damning MSG studies were published, and I'd wondered whether Doritos were simply a drug-delivery system, stimulating appetites in the brain, hooking unsuspecting third graders, causing rampant headaches and obesity. One of my ex-wife Peggy's parting shots had been that FL was no better than Philip Morris. But Helen, by sheer force of personality, had countered Peggy's negativity and largely restored my faith, and my snack-to-meal concept that afternoon had been a sort of offering to her, a renewal of my commitment to the brand.

Yet I drove home from work that day in a bit of a funk. I was afraid I'd made a fool of myself in front of Helen with my meal idea. Why hadn't I stuck to supporting the flavoring visions of others? Why had I spent so much time and money on vitamin adhesion before knowing it was a go? Why had I bluntly tried to lead when it was my nature to follow?

I arrived at my two-bedroom ranch on Debbie Drive in East Plano, where I had lived since Peggy asked me to leave six years earlier. Peggy and I were from Milwaukee, and she wasn't happy about moving to Texas, an attitude that only intensified as she raised our two children in Plano while I worked absurd hours for Frito-Lay. As her resentments grew, she used her sexual availability, or lack thereof, to punish me. For instance, if I stayed later than eight at work, I could count on coming home to find her already in bed, sometimes snuggling with our youngest, Ashley. By the time I told her about things that were bothering me, they'd been festering for too long. Unfortunately, there's no apologizing for saying certain things in a certain tone.

Now I went straight to the cupboard and popped a new thirteen-ounce bag of Salsa Doritos. This was always a special moment for me: the released air was a breath from the manufacturing facility itself, an atmospheric postcard from the place of the product's creation. I ate the chips like a chain-smoker, reaching for a fresh one, preferably unbroken, as soon as I had chewed the previous, pausing only to drink from a bottle of cherry soda. It might be said that my taste in food was suffering from arrested development, but I wanted to live in my field as deeply as I could.

I ended up consuming over half of the Doritos while preparing spaghetti sauce spiked with dangerous amounts of Lawry's. By the time supper was ready, I didn't feel like eating. After a few forkfuls of pasta, I rinsed my mouth and brushed my teeth, preparing myself for a night of surfing for porn.

In the wake of my divorce, I had taken compulsive solace in sexual images of people I did not know. My sex life and my love life had gone their separate ways, with my sex life happening inches from the computer and my love life essentially not happening at all. What would Janice Howard say if she learned I spent my leisure time in this way? Probably, "It figures." Or, "That's consistent with his aggressiveness in meetings." Or, "This man should be banned from making food for other people. It's disgusting to think that a man with such prurient tastes for women has been inflicting his flavors on unsuspecting snack eaters around the globe."

It occurred to me, as I pondered these judgments, that while Americans had overcome the challenges inherent in producing quality snacks, we were not as good at fostering quality human relationships; in fact, it seemed that the pursuit of instant gratification, in all its forms, from snacks to porn, might keep people from really getting to know each other. It also occurred to me briefly, as briefly as flying past a station where your train does not stop, that I myself—once a normal-seeming, high-achieving, up-with-life kind of guy—had arrived at a state of near soullessness. Then I headed for the computer.

I surfed diligently, one browser window open to still thumbnail sites, where I clicked through "hardcore" and "big boobs," another browser checking out the movie sites. I was looking for something to start my motor, but nothing worked. It seemed I had already seen all these bodies. Why, I wondered, was it important to see this woman's shaved crotch? Why should fitting those genitals together be sexy? Was that someone's anus? Why?

I gave up and moped about the house, did the dishes, and stood at the kitchen sink, staring at the backyard. There were empty bird feeders out there, tall plastic tubes with perches and holes, hanging on hooks from thin metal rods. They'd been left by the previous owner, and it had never occurred to me to fill them with bird food. I didn't understand the point of bird watching. I had no idea where the pleasure in that came from.

At that instant, a bird alighted on one of the feeders, and then, just like that, it was gone again. The empty feeder was left swaying.

I said aloud: "Hello, Helen? It's me, Reggie."

Maybe it was Mike's comment about the door closing, or maybe it was the sense that I needed to break a fall of some kind, but in any case, the next thing I knew, months of excuses and years of self-doubt were slipping away: I was calling Helen at her home, asking her out for a drink that very evening.

Her pause of consideration was dramatic. Finally she said, "Sure, why not?"

.   .   .

"You think I made an ass of myself today?" I asked Helen from my captain's chair in the bar at Bennigan's.

"No, you were fine. We've got some work to do, though, I'll say that."

She had changed into jeans that looked ironed and a white blouse with the sleeves rolled up so precisely they made her seem buttoned-up, not casual.

"So you've really been with FL for over twenty-five years?" she asked.

I nodded, then asked, "Do you think what we do is valuable, in a larger sense? Do you think it makes people truly happy?" I had no idea what to talk to her about, but I was genuinely curious about this question.

"In our corner of the consumer staples space," she said, "people don't buy something unless it makes them happy, and people buy a lot of our product."

I couldn't tell whether she believed what she'd said or if she was simply in VP mode. She was one of the most controlled, unflappable people I had ever met. At that moment, I conceived my desire to have sex with her as a way to tap into her power.

"You could say we're in the happiness business," I affirmed.

"Yes, you could say that." She smiled at me. I smiled at her.

"What are you drinking again?" I asked. "Let me get you another one."

. . .

After her fourth Jameson, she loosened up considerably. The precise dimensions of her bitterness toward her ex-husband became clear. Her two boys, Trevor and Jeremy, fourteen and sixteen respectively, had apparently chosen to stay with this defective man in Cincinnati. I didn't say a single disparaging word about Peggy. My theory was that women didn't want to listen to a guy who thought negatively about any woman.

When we finally left, I walked her to her car and impulsively gave her a sloppy kiss, bending her back against the driver-side door of her Lexus SUV.

"You're full of piss and vinegar, aren't you, Reggie?" she slurred. Over her whiskey breath, I got a strong whiff of a Southside Chicago accent I hadn't heard before. "You're a fun guy. You should call me some time."

"I did call you," I said.

This made us laugh like a pair of hopeless drunks, but it was still wonderful. Life was suddenly plumped for the taking again, like a huge pineapple.

. . .

Soon after that night, Helen and I lunched, we movied. I put myself on a crash diet and began jogging. At any moment, I believed, spontaneous magic could break out and Helen would see my entire body uncovered. Despite the passion of our first kiss, however, she'd seemed in no rush to get me into bed. So much the better, I thought.

Team Doritos went about its business. New jalapeño-related concepts were afoot, and, surprisingly, Helen discreetly funneled money to me for vitamin research. Three weeks after Helen and I first kissed, Janice did in fact file her weight discrimination lawsuit. Using as examples four other heavy women and two men in various jobs in the Plano headquarters alone, her lawyers argued there was a "systematic pattern of discrimination, built on unfair and destructive stereotypes of large people as 'out of control,' 'sleepy,' and 'obsessed with eating rather than working.'" Her claims were bolstered by studies charting the perfectly normal work performance of heavy people. Moreover, Frito-Lay was accused of being grossly hypocritical by encouraging the consumption of fattening snacks while "tying a glass belt" around the careers of heavies.

Helen gave me all of this legal dope over the phone, swearing me to secrecy.

She said, "We might have to lay low for a bit, you and me."

"I understand."

"Janice is on the warpath. If she thinks we're dating, she'll say I'm abusing my power and gumming up the process of the development team."

"I like your power," I said. "It turns me on."

"That's nice, Reggie."

"I mean, it's not really a suit against you, is it?"

She sighed. "Well, the suit talks about me being hired instead of Janice, though it doesn't put me at risk, per se. But Janice is tough. She's got a lot of clout in the company, and I'm in her sights."

"Hey, you want me to rough her up, teach her some manners?"

Helen's laugh was hollow. At that moment, she seemed more exhausted than I'd been when I'd worked those unconscionable hours—only to come home to find Peggy asleep.

At the office, Helen maintained her steely poise. Perhaps only I noticed the signs of strain. Janice herself was defiantly piling it on in the employee cafeteria, maybe daring someone to make a comment that would play into her litigious hands, and her normal bluff heartiness seemed turned up a notch to show how confident and unstressed she was. Then Helen's son Jeremy was in a dirt-bike accident back in Cincinnati, and she was out for a few days visiting him. When she got back, she surprised me by inviting me to her house for dinner.

"Double back a few times," she said, "to make sure no one's following you."

.   .   .

Helen had purchased a home north of Plano, past 121, nearly out among the cotton fields, in a brand new development: the Villas at Running Trees Estates. Except for a smattering of old hickories, the whole neighborhood was fresh out of the box. Concrete streets were pristine, curbs immaculate. Underground, no doubt, miles of white PVC pipe obediently carried away excrement.

The first sign of Helen herself was her silver Lexus standing in the driveway. I parked my Saturn beside it. The facade of her house was extremely complicated, with sections of stone, frosted red brick, bay windows, a lancet window, columns, an oriel, battlements, cornices, gables, fanlight windows, and portals. And the place was huge, probably five thousand square feet.

She greeted me wearing a sleeveless blue top, white Capri pants, and sandals. I was dressed like a golf cart salesman in tan khaki pants, loafers, and a brandless red short-sleeved shirt. We might have created a small tornado right there on her front porch, with her air-conditioning rushing out against May's heat.

"Don't just stand there like the mailman," she said, "come on in." She waved a bare muscular arm, and I followed.

Of course it was a two-story entryway, lit by a fanlight window and, higher up, by a portal. The floors were marble—I could sense their coolness even through my loafers. To the right, receding into the distance, was the enormous sunken living room filled with plants and swooping curves of dark purple sectional furniture forming obscure symbols like some kind of silent marching band. The living room had also required two stories, with several floor-to-ceiling windows along one wall and a balcony leading to some other wing of the house.

"There's a good place to give a speech," I said, pointing to the balcony.

"What was that?" Helen asked with her back to me, already striding down a corridor. Apparently she was wearing a pair of those hi-tech panties that leave no discernible lines.

"Ah, nothing," I said. "This is a helluva house."

She led me back to an expansive kitchen, where, waiting for us on an island, were a clear glass bowl of Tostitos Scoops and a smaller clear glass bowl of salsa. Instinctively and without invitation, I tested the products. It was our own salsa, medium.

"You want a beer?" she asked.

"Most definitely."

She found a Corona for me and poured white wine for herself. I held the Corona politely until she raised her glass of wine. "Cheers," she said.

"Cheers," I said. We clinked. "How's Jeremy?" I asked.

"Fine. Recovering well. John thinks it'll make a man out of him," she said, her voice as dry as Amarillo.

"Hmmm," I said, not sure whether egging her on about her ex would be a good thing. I took a huge swig of my beer.

"Listen," she said, "I hate to talk shop, but with this lawsuit and everything, there's some stuff I've been meaning to ask you."

"Sure, that's fine," I said, caught off guard but flattered all the same.

"What do you know about Janice's relationship with Nancy Sargent?"

I had to think for a bit. "Well, I know Janice once introduced Nancy for a speech at the annual motivation banquet," I said. "Like a year or two before you got here. And Janice said she preferred calling Nancy our 'elder' or 'wise woman,' instead of president."

"How did Nancy take that?"

"I think she bought it. Janice is really good with head honchos. She's one of those kiss-up-and-piss-down types." I was afraid I'd said too much, but I'd been starving myself in my final push toward svelteness, and the beer had gone straight to my head.

Yet Helen went on to ask me about the director of Human Resources, Megan Coughlin, and as I answered more of her questions about our colleagues, she seemed to take up each detail like a sandbag, shifting it in her mind, deciding exactly where she would put it down to protect herself. I began to believe I was more valuable to her as a source on office politics than as a man who had been diligently toning his body to better serve her during lovemaking.

Finally she reached out a hand and clasped my upper arm, the way a guy might do. "Sorry about all that," she said. "Now we can relax and have some dinner." She smiled and we sat down to a meal—chicken cordon bleu—that was uneventful until we got around to how strange it was that both of us had exes and kids in the Midwest.

"It is weird," I said. "I hear about Ashley and Ryan and talk to them, and we visit sometimes, but I wonder if I should have put up more of a fight when Peggy wanted to move back to Milwaukee."

"Don't beat yourself up, Reggie," Helen said. "We need you down here."

"I haven't been the world's greatest dad," I persisted glumly. The kids had actually given me a "World's Greatest Dad" coffee mug for Father's Day. I came home late from work one night that winter with a bad sore throat. I wanted to make some tea in that cup, but I couldn't find it anywhere. Most likely Peggy had disappeared the mug.

"Come on, Reg," Helen said. "Let it go."

She got up and started to clear the table, which was fine, I told myself, because I didn't want to be a Gloomy Gus with her.

After we both piled our dishes in the sink, Helen asked, "Do you want a tour?"

"Sure," I said.

She showed me the rest of the first floor and took me out onto a deck. There was seating for twelve people out there; the umbrella on the table was down; just beyond the deck was a small pool with the cover on it.

"No bird feeders?" I asked.

"Pardon?"

"I was just noticing you don't seem to like bird feeders."

"No," she said. "The way I see it, they'd be inhumane. I mean, if I had some, the damned birds would come to rely on them. And I don't have the time to keep refilling them."

"So you've considered them."

"Yes. I suppose I have."

Then she led me upstairs, where we passed several bedrooms. It started to seem as if this was the moment I'd been preparing myself for. As Helen energetically praised the mother-of-pearl inlays on the whirlpool fixtures in the guest bathroom, I imagined the tub filling with pure dopamine.

Then we entered the master bedroom, and she took my hand. I felt the onrush of sexual arousal. The wall overlooking the backyard was curved outward.

"That's an incredible view," I said, trying to distract Helen from the tent in my khakis.

Her fingers tugged mine, and we sat on the bed. She kicked off her sandals. I slipped off my loafers and let my feet tuck them behind the coverlet, and the phone rang.

On the fourth ring, she said, "Mind if I get that?"

"No, that's fine."

She twisted around to grab the phone.

"Hello?" she said. "Oh, hi."

Why now? I thought.

"Jesus Christ," she said. "Jesus."

She glanced at me briefly as she listened.

"It's terrible, and I don't know what to think," she said. "That's OK. I'm glad you called. I'll see you Monday." The other person said more things. "I know. I'll call you. . . That's all right. Bye."

She hung up and stood and looked out the window. "I can't believe this," she said. "Janice—she had a heart attack."

Impossible, I thought. "Is she all right?" I asked.

"No."

"Is she alive?"

"No. She's gone."

I allowed myself to consider those last two words, to let them settle into me as well as they could. I wondered if a part of Helen was glad, but then told myself I might not yet have the right to know that. She turned from the window and looked at her bed, her hands on her cheeks, apparently working to resolve some lengthening chain of thought.

"I hate to say this," I said, "but I feel a little relieved." I heard how this sounded, then ran my fingers through my hair. "I mean, for you, too," I said. "I mean, for us."

She looked up and stared at me, then faced the curved window. I thought of comforting her, physically, maybe putting a consoling arm around her, though I was not exactly sure how this was done. I stood up and sort of wavered toward her.

She took a step away from me. "That's sweet, Reggie," she said. "You're actually a sweet guy. But I'd really like to be alone right now. OK?"

I wondered if she was asking me to leave simply because she was freaked out by Janice's death, or because she no longer needed me to help defend herself. Maybe I had been taste-tested and found wanting.

"OK," I said. I stepped into my loafers, nodded good-bye, and let myself out of her house.

.   .   .

As I drove away from the Villas at Running Trees Estates, Janice's death sat heavily on my mind, but I wouldn't say I was grieving for her; the feeling was more general. I stopped at Tom Thumb to replenish my stock of Taco. I imagined eating the entire bag of chips on the way home and then spending the rest of the night with the computer. The prospect of returning to such pleasures came with a strong undertow of regret.

As I slid the bag on the express lane conveyor belt, the sun-burned clerk asked, "Find everything?"

"As matter of fact, no," I said. "Do you have any birdseed?"

"Pet supplies," she said. "Aisle ten?"

This wasn't too far from where I stood. "Let me run and get a bag," I said.

I honed right in on it. Back at the checkout, I said, "Now I won't get my eyes pecked out if I set foot on the back porch."

She rang up both items, and as I stuffed the change into my pocket, I remembered the only other time I'd felt birdseed in my hands. It was at a wedding of one of Peggy's cousins, the last wedding Peggy and I went to before the divorce. We threw birdseed at the couple as they left the church. This was when everyone thought rice would make birds explode. As a food scientist, I had good reasons to consider this phenomenon extremely unlikely and, on the drive to the reception, I'd fallen into a casual argument about it with Peggy's brother, then a sort of front-seat cage match with Peggy herself, and she told me that if I didn't spend so much freaking time in the lab flavoring insidious corn chips, I'd know what really mattered on a day like this.

Now, alone in that same car, I resisted cracking open the Doritos. It took a staggering effort not to eat them as I drove, as I had done many times in the past. Maybe Janice's death somehow exemplified Peggy's criticism; maybe Helen's rebuff cast oblique doubt on the brand.

But the more I thought about things, the better I grasped the simple but profound ideas that had been driving me all this time. I had wanted to make quality snacks that could be eaten with lunch, or after hearty recreation or a tough day at the office, or at holiday parties, picnics, or any truly special occasion—a birthday, a wedding shower, even a wake: snacks that would always be a part of sustenance and joy and consolation. Quality snacks and quality relationships were not opposed but complementary, because snacks eased relationships—hadn't chips and salsa helped Helen and me to converse this very evening?—and relationships in turn provided occasions for snacks. And when relationships failed or death struck, snacks were still there. No one could dispute this fact.

So, in the end, was it so wrong to imagine, and to live by the notion, that if people had the best snacks available, they could make it through just about anything?

Yet after I was safely inside my house, I still didn't open those Doritos. Standing in my kitchen, I faced my modestly sized window. It was dark out there. I flicked on the back porch light and took the birdseed outside and filled the feeders to their brims. This wasn't as easy as it looked, and I spilled a fair amount on the lawn.

"Birds of all feathers?" I said quietly. "Enjoy these snacks."

Then I went back inside, where I held onto the edge of my kitchen sink, leaning toward the window, as if waiting for the birds to arrive. I wanted to see them as soon as possible, to observe them and what they did, and understand why it was important to watch them.

Self-Reliance

After Ronald Reagan became president, hard times found me in West Allis, Wisconsin. They followed me around, then they got ahead of me—like my shadow. The sun flew into the air every morning but crossed the sky low and to the south, like a wobbly punt that curved out-of-bounds. A wrecking ball was knocking down six-blocks worth of Allis-Chalmers. Twenty-foot-tall dump trucks hauled off the rubble. Some debris went by train. Borden's still made milk and sherbet and ice cream at the plant on Highway 100, and Elsie the Cow's red-and-yellow face still smiled that sure-I'll-have-some-milk! smile from the side of the building, but I had been laid off from Borden's—this time for good, it seemed—and was trying to make it delivering pizzas three nights a week at Todd's Pizza Mountain.

Then something happened at a New Year's Eve party. It was at a fancy condo in Bishop's Woods. I barely knew the people. Dwayne knew them. Dwayne was my best friend. We worked in the ice-cream freezers together, lived together, chased women together, and got laid off the past September together. He'd met Stephanie at The Happy Tap last summer after a softball game. She was a softball groupie. "Bring the whole team," she'd told Dwayne.

Dwayne insisted we go to two other parties first, so we didn't get to Stephanie's until two in the morning. They had one of those blue siren lights going in the living room, and Prince's "1999" was shaking the place. The revolving light slipped over lamps and pictures and the couple making out on the couch. I turned to tell Dwayne that the light and sound were like two hands feeling up the room, but he'd disappeared. I wandered around—the sunroom, the kitchen—running into little groups of people I didn't know.

I caught up with Dwayne in one of the bedrooms. He had Stephanie against the wall and they were kissing like mad. They broke it off—or I should say, Stephanie broke it off—when I came into the room.

"Happy New Year!" she said. She gave me a weird lewd drunken smile, but like she knew she was doing it. I smiled back and winked for good measure. Once I'd talked to her at The Happy Tap after a game. She was sarcastic, but I liked her. She had a habit of saying "sounds like a good time" without meaning it. Now she said, "Happy New Year" again. She kissed me on the mouth, then deeper.

"Do you have a friend?" Dwayne asked her.

Dwayne always got the good-looking one, I always got the friend, the "ugly" one. I didn't mind. She was usually nicer. She'd be real nervous and sweat through her perfume, and then you could smell what she was really like.

But there was no friend tonight, so I kept kissing Stephanie with my eyes half closed. I could hear Dwayne's hands moving across the fabric of her dress, her dress sliding against her body. I thought I was touching her where I was touching her *and* where he was touching her. Sometimes we'd meet a pair of women and end up on opposite sides of the living room at the apartment, but we'd never been with the same girl before. Then Dwayne pulled on her and I let her go.

"Much later," Dwayne said to me, his fingers on the spaghetti straps of her dress.

But she said, "I want him here."

"Come on, Steph."

"Let him stay—I want to do it this time." She talked in a secret pouty voice, but I could hear everything.

Dwayne said no way.

Stephanie slipped out of his arms and pulled her straps up. "Happy New Year," she said and wobbled for the door.

Old Dwayne cursed and shot her an icy glare—the way he looked at the next batter after someone had just tagged a home run off him—but he seemed too horny to negotiate. "All right," he said to her, "come on. Let's go."

He pulled her to him, tipped her onto the bed, and lay on top of her. I shut the door and took off my shoes and jeans. I couldn't decide whether the lamp on the nightstand should be off or on. I turned it off, but then it seemed too dark, so I turned it back on.

"What the hell is wrong with you?" Dwayne grunted.

I laughed at myself and finished undressing. They had undressed more quickly, and Dwayne entered her doggy-style, as if he wanted to keep her between us.

I finally crawled onto the bed. Stephanie's face was near the headboard, her hair hanging down. There wasn't much room for me to be in front of her, and I wondered if Dwayne had done this on purpose.

I kissed the side of her face through her hair. She turned to me and kissed me softly on the mouth and then trailed her lips up my cheek. "Sixty-nine," she whispered in my ear.

I couldn't tell if she was serious or joking, so I lay on my back across the top of the bed, perpendicular to Dwayne and Stephanie, and Stephanie kissed me from above, her hair falling down my cheeks and neck. We did this for a long time—it really got me going. I almost forgot about sixty-nining until she whispered a reminder. Then while I was twisting my hips over, pivoting on my shoulders, trying to travel headfirst down Stephanie's body so as to sneak up on where the two of them were joined, my dick got surprisingly close to my own mouth.

"Hey, that's not for you," she said.

"I know that."

"I bet he can suck his own dick," she giggled over her shoulder.

"He better not," Dwayne said, puffing a little. The bed was rocking.

"I never have," I said. "I never knew."

"If you suck your dick here, man, I'm going to kill you," Dwayne said. "As soon as I'm done."

At that point, the old sixty-nine no longer seemed an option. Dwayne and I ended up facing each other, kneeling at opposite ends of Stephanie. It was strange and exciting—with the power of a famous historical moment on TV. Dwayne closed his eyes or looked at Stephanie's hips the whole time. When she finished me with her hand, I shot clean over her shoulder and got some on Dwayne. It took him forever after that, and when he finally came his face looked like a bee was stinging him in the ass.

I thought Stephanie was maybe too drunk to come. As Dwayne and I were getting dressed, she was still lying facedown on the bed, her right hand groping around like she'd lost something. She made me think of the difference between getting laid and getting laid off. I wanted to give her another chance.

I started to slide my jeans down again, but Dwayne grabbed my arm. "That's enough, Lover Boy." He buckled his belt and business was officially closed for the night.

We walked through the sharp, cold air to where Dwayne's car was parked in a lot surrounded by snow and woods. Dwayne wasn't talking.

"Sorry about jizzing on you," I said, "and sticking around, too."

"Doesn't matter. I was getting tired of her anyway." He opened the driver-side door, grabbed the scraper, and threw it to me. While the car warmed up, I scratched frost off the windows. Dwayne sat behind the wheel with his hands between his legs, his chin tucked in his collar, his eyes staring at the dash.

We tooled up and down the hills of Elm Grove Road, past The Red Mill where Dwayne and I sometimes took women for fish fry, past Linfield where we went to grade school and where Dwayne was the king of full-court murderball.

"Remember last year?" Dwayne said.

"Not really."

"Now *that* was a great party." Dwayne made a gesture with his right hand that reminded me of the Statue of Liberty. "Me and Cheryl—man! I'll never forget that."

Cheryl was Dwayne's steady for two whole months, until she wanted a rock.

Nostalgia in a guy like Dwayne is never a good sign. I thought I'd bring him up-to-date with a humorous story.

"Hey, remember that ad in the *Journal* for the forklift operator at Krueger? I forgot to tell you what happened. About a thousand guys showed up but it turned out some guy put through a two-year-old job req by accident." I laughed a start-up laugh.

"I'm sick of getting fucked over."

Dwayne wasn't moaning over nothing. UPS didn't need anyone, the breweries didn't need anyone. Allis-Chalmers would never need anyone again. We couldn't do what they needed at Allen-Bradley. That went for a bunch of places. I was lucky to get my job at Todd's Pizza Mountain. Meanwhile, I was checking out every men's department in the Milwaukee metropolitan area, trying to become a salesman. I hadn't had a single decent interview. A matter of appearance, I thought.

"Have you ever thought of selling men's clothing?" I asked Dwayne. "You sort of look like a mannequin."

"Listen, I'm not working any job where I have to tell other guys their seat is too tight or their crotch is too low, or shit like that."

"I'd like it. Especially working on commission. You'd sort of be your own boss. The better you do, the more money you get. Can't get laid off if you're self-employed."

"They could still fire you," Dwayne said, racing down 124th Street. Then he gave me a look like he just noticed I had a horn on my forehead. "You *would* like it. I hear about you sucking your dick, I'm moving out. I'm not living with a fag."

"Everybody masturbates."

"Christ, Rudy! Do you always have to come out and *say* shit like that? Jesus."

Maybe I'd gone too far. Like the time a bunch of us were over at Red Carpet Lanes, and I said that it'd be great if we kept score just by writing down the feelings we had as the ball rolled toward the pins. It was one of those moments when you feel people looking at you and you think, "Are they for me or against me?" It's not a great moment.

.   .   .

New Year's Day we got tanked on beer and chips and watched the Rose Bowl. The game was a seesaw battle. Every Michigan touchdown had Dwayne throwing his fist in the air, and then holding his palm up so we could high-five. Every USC score confused and angered him. "Fuck!" he'd yell.

I was rooting for Michigan as well. I couldn't resist a team named the "Wolverines."

When Michigan lost, Dwayne broke his hand on the coffee table.

"Fuck! I bet two hundred bucks on that game!" He cradled his hand and groaned. His face was twisted just like the face of an injured Michigan player who'd been pulled out of the game. I thought of pointing this out to Dwayne, but it was hard to talk over his howling and swearing.

I hustled him to the emergency room, but then I had to rush off to work. He resented that. After they set his bones in order, I picked him up on the way to one of my deliveries and took him home. He got me in trouble by opening the box and grabbing a piece of pizza as he bailed out of the car. Todd always said, "No friends in the delivery car."

"Some friend," I thought, as the bastard made off with the slice.

.　.　.

Being unemployed had understandably put a bug up Dwayne's ass. But even with medical bills on the way, he kept living the high life, wining and dining the ladies, loading his credit cards. Finally I had to let him go out by himself sometimes, because I didn't have the cash, even though I was dying to find a girl who would go with my new trick, a girl with a certain look in the eye.

The odd thing was, even though we'd been laid off for months, I was dreaming more and more about the ice-cream freezer, mainly variations on one dream where I was made to wear an embarrassing hairdo. I would try to undo it, but it was frozen. On warm-up break, it would almost thaw out—sometimes I could even work with it a little—but the bell always dinged and I had to go back in. The freezer would be deserted. I'd search for people up and down the frosty aisles, but I always ended up trying to look in a tub of ice cream. My fingers would freeze to the lid and then I knew I was caught and then I'd wake up.

Dwayne said my dreams showed a secret desire to be trapped and frozen to death. I said the opposite, and we also argued about what the embarrassing hairdo meant. Then I came home from the Pizza Mountain one Saturday night in late February and all of Dwayne's stuff was gone. He had just packed up and left. No note or anything. We were behind on phone, gas, electric, and rent. I'd put the bills out for him to put in his check, but those envelopes were still stuck to the refrigerator with magnets. The last phone bill had a lot of Los Angeles calls on it. He'd told me once that in LA it was very easy to get beautiful women, plus there was no winter to cut into ice-cream consumption. Maybe he went to California, was all I could think. I didn't know what to do, so I went into my room, took off my pants, flipped my hips over my head, and sucked my own dick.

Monday night I went to Todd's Pizza Mountain knowing I needed at least another shift. When I got back from the last delivery of dinner rush, Todd was sitting at the little table in front that customers sometimes waited at, staring at the traffic on Highway 100. His paper hat was tipped way back. Even with his lion-colored mustache he looked more like a skinny busboy than a businessman pushing forty. His Pizza Mountain was crushed between a Greek restaurant and a barbershop—a slot with some counters, an oven, a sink. The tiny marquee letters on the menu board said, "Try our Special, Super Special, and Deluxe Super Special." I'd been thinking we got along all right. I'd imagined telling him what a reliable worker I was, how with him making and me delivering we could build this place. We could turn heads over at the West Allis Chamber of Commerce.

"Not a bad night," I said, taking a seat. "For a Monday."

"A little slow, a little slow."

"That's because it's a Monday. How about a Friday? How about Monday, Wednesday, Friday, Saturday? Just one more night. Come on."

"This isn't General Motors," he said.

"You do a decent business. All's I'm asking is—"

"Rudy, I'd love to, I really would." He put his forearms on the table, leaned at me. "But who am I supposed to cut? Dennis has two kids. Then where's Dennis? Tim's in trouble. Where's Tim?"

"Tim makes his own trouble." We both knew Tim had a gambling problem.

There must've been something in my face or the way I said it, but Todd did a double take. "Listen, if I could do more for you, I would, but I can't. I thought you wanted to sell clothes, anyways?"

"I don't know where my career is headed right now," I said foolishly.

The phone rang and Todd got up to take the order. It occurred to me that I had entirely forgotten what I'd planned on saying to him about my reliability, about our future.

"Midway Motor Lodge." He ripped the ticket from the pad and headed back to make the pizza. I asked him if it was a man or a woman, and he said a woman—with an accent.

I perked up. Delivering to motels always made me horny. Motel people were lonely, they drank, they offered you things. When he hired me, Todd had said that every delivery guy who'd put in serious time with him had gotten into "something interesting" on a delivery. "Who needs benefits!" he'd said.

Things were looking good when Todd told me the woman

wanted me to stop for a six-pack on my way to the Motor Lodge, but the person who opened the door to 211 was a man.

The man was dressed in black. His shirt was unbuttoned all the way, and his thin stomach was swirled with dark hair. He had about an eight-day beard and a pointy chin.

"Come in," he said. His accent was sort of Russian but not quite. "Rita, pay him."

He went to sit at the end of the bed, picked up a camera—a fancy-looking one—and started taking pictures of what was happening on TV. I thought this was kind of strange.

Rita came out of the bathroom. She wore a man's white dress shirt tucked in and brown jeans that had the back pockets ripped off and little zippers at the ankles. She was barefoot. Her dark eyes seemed distressed. Whatever her troubles might be, I wanted to help her solve them.

The man saw me staring at her bent over her purse and he smiled in a smug way. I was embarrassed and looked away. She waved a traveler's check. It was probably all right to take it, but I shook my head. I was in no hurry. When she didn't argue with me, I was surprised. She said something to the man in a foreign language, but I knew it had to do with not having money.

He ignored her and took another picture of the TV.

"Are you a photographer?" I asked him. I was never afraid to ask an obvious question.

He jerked his head at Rita. "*Porn*ographer." He grinned at me. I could tell he took me for an idiot, but I wasn't sure what that meant about what he'd said.

She cursed him in their language and rifled through a duffel bag.

I put the pizza and six-pack on a low dresser. I became aware of my throat.

"You brought us beer," he said. "Very nice. Rita said it was illegal, extra charge. Why don't you have one? Throw one to me."

I did this. His brown eyes were very small.

"'Illegal' surprised me," he went on. "I came to this country to avoid 'illegal.'"

"We don't have a liquor license, is all. Is pornography illegal in your country?"

"Sure, sure. So you see, I had to come." He raised his hands as if he'd had no choice at all and smiled hard. He opened his beer and guzzled from it. Then I opened mine and did the same.

Rita put in her two cents, in their language, shaking her head, now back to her purse, paging through big, colorful bills.

He put his beer on the carpet and took pictures of the TV screen again. With each click, I couldn't help but imagine Rita posed in a different position.

"Do you make movies, too?" I said.

"Ah, films. Not so many now, but who knows."

Rita said something fierce to him. Maybe she was embarrassed about him bringing up his pornography. With just a few singles crushed in her hand, she dumped the purse on the bed in disgust and strode toward the windows, passing in front of the man. He patted her on the butt and smiled. Rita rummaged through a suitcase lying open against the wall.

The man snapped another picture of the TV. "Yes," he said, satisfied with the shot. It was three guys riding horses out west.

He picked up his beer and let the camera dangle from his neck. "So she is beautiful?" he said, referring to Rita, and took another swig. His eyes still watched me as he drank.

I nodded silently. This man had a way of making me feel I'd known him for a long time—even that I owed him money or something—but I liked where this was going. He lifted his chin a little. The small brown foreign eyes saw something in me.

"I have a talent," I said.

He nodded, expecting to hear exactly this. He spoke to the woman in their language and laughed, as if everybody had a talent.

She said the equivalent of "ta-da" and was holding the cash. The man turned toward me and put out his hand to stop her.

"What is your talent?"

"You can hire actors for your movies, can't you?" I was being very careful.

"Sure, sure," he said quickly, a little irritated with me.

Rita scolded him in their language, her hands on her hips.

He snapped at her, so meanly that my eyes locked onto his eyes. I took his side in their argument, only because I thought it would bring me to Rita in the long run.

Rita threw up her hands. She appealed to a god. I could tell that.

"We have studios," he went on in a quiet voice, looking at me intently. "We have studios in California. We are always looking for new talent. What is your talent?"

I wanted to tell him, but I couldn't. "It's embarrassing," I breathed.

"No," he said. "Your talent is your soul. You must be proud."

"I want to be proud," I said. I looked to Rita, who avoided my eyes.

"Then tell me," the man said. "Don't be shy."

"All right," I said, my heart starting to beat in my ears. I looked nowhere in the room: "I can suck my own dick."

He whistled soft and low. "Impossible," he said. Rita put her hand to her mouth, as if she were about to sneeze.

"I've done it," I said.

"I don't believe you." He picked up his camera and took another picture of the TV. I saw myself leaving that room and getting into my car and driving back to Todd's Pizza Mountain, my tip a few coins of change if they even had enough for the whole bill.

"I can prove it," I said.

He lowered his camera and stared at me. "He says he can prove," he said, as if he was speaking to Rita, but he didn't take his eyes off of me.

She slapped him on the shoulder and swore. He ignored her. He had hypnotist's eyes and he knew it. "So prove," he said. "And maybe I pay you extra, huh?"

"How much?"

He made a clown frown and nodded his head from side to side. "Five dollars," he finally said.

"I am looking for work," I said, looking right back into his eyes. "Sir, I really hope that if you are pleased by my demonstration, you will give me a *ten* dollar tip—plus a job. I'll follow you to California in my car. Sir, I am very serious about this."

Rita appealed to a god again.

A small part of the man's smile came back. "OK, let's stop this fucking around. OK? Go on. Prove."

I took a long drink of beer and set the can down on the dresser with a trembling hand. It seemed my time had come. Dropping my pants, I felt like a con escaping from jail, taking off my orange jumpsuit. I was sweating a lot under my arms. I touched my skin and my fingers were ice cold. I was shivering.

Rita whispered to the man in a quick urgent voice, but he shushed her.

When I was naked except for my T-shirt, I crawled onto the bed. I stared at Rita, her face, her breasts, the gathering of cloth in her crotch. I swung my legs over my head and went into the position. I moved my leg so it would block the man from my view, but so that

I could see Rita through my legs. Because of the angle, I could only see her face, her sweet, confused face, which was turned away. It reminded me of some of the second-rate faces my various friends had had, but I loved these faces. These people all had to have a lot of inner resources to make it with second-string looks. I respected that.

I got my dick in my mouth and went at it. The man took pictures. A gunfight broke out on the TV. Rita stepped away to where I couldn't see her. I thought she might be getting undressed to join me in my audition, which would be the first in a famous career. Maybe gay films, but I didn't think like Dwayne. I thought anyone would be interested in seeing a sexual feat. Or maybe I'd branch out and do the straight-ahead stuff and only do my trick by myself, at the end, as the credits were rolling. We would all live in California, where Dwayne was. I would leave the apartment and the bills just as Dwayne had. I sucked my own dick. I was really going at it.

At first I must not have even noticed the laughter. I only really heard it when it was going full blast, when the man was slapping his thigh and sucking air in a spastic rhythm and Rita was giggling hysterically. Then I saw her face hanging over me. It reminded me of Stephanie's hovering face and how much I had loved kissing her, and for an unbelievable instant I thought Rita still might join me. But her cheeks were streaked with tears of laughter. In a soft accent that killed me, she said, "We are so sorry. We are not pornos. Tibor—he has bad sense of humor."

I looked into her mouth. For a second, I could see the bottoms of her two wet front teeth; then her lips closed like curtains. I looked at my shrinking dick. "That's OK," I murmured.

.　　.　　.

If you took off all of your skin so that the surface of your body was just a land of nerves, you would try to be completely still, because even a little air blowing on you—maybe just the air moving between the rooms of a house, or the tiny wind you make when you turn your head—might be enough to make you scream bloody murder. When I was getting dressed, I tried to hold myself still like that. I kept telling myself I didn't know these people, I'd never see them again. But as still as I was, just the warmth from their bodies raked my open nerves. I could hear the sounds of a scream echoing inside my head like a yell from deep in the freezer.

Gradually, though, I got numb. I remembered Stephanie face-down on the bed, maybe fighting off the spins. Why had she taken on both of us that night? Was she needling Dwayne? Or looking for humiliation? Or just trying to come?

Up close, Rita's face showed damage. She put money in my hands. Tibor sat and stared at the TV. "Good-bye, Tibor," I said. "Good-bye, Rita."

I closed their door with a soft click and walked down the hall, trying to figure out what had happened. Yes, they had seen everything about me, but it occurred to me that you can't rely on yourself if you feel ashamed of yourself, so I told myself I was not ashamed. I thought I could even go back and sit and talk with Rita and Tibor—and it wouldn't matter. I wondered how anyone could possibly fear relations with other humans. I wondered how humiliation worked because I couldn't imagine that emotion anymore.

I guess I'm saying that all I had left was a strong feeling. It was a Mary Tyler Moore feeling, a you're-gonna-make-it-after-all feeling. I saw a light on under another door. I knocked.

"Who is it?" a woman's muffled voice said.

"Pizza man," I said. Deception seemed necessary, and now I would do what was necessary, but I couldn't actually lie.

The door to 219 opened, pulling the chain tight. Part of a middle-aged woman's face appeared, in the gap.

Our eyes met as she moved her head to take me in.

"I've come to set you free," I said.

She slammed the door.

But I thought positively. I was self-reliant. The self-reliant man relies on himself not to give up. The self-reliant man does not fear rejection. He is useful to himself at all times.

I went down the hall, looking for light under the doors.

Woman of Peace

By the time she turned seventeen, Meg Shannon had come to believe that the world pretty much sucked, but with the help of friends and family you could build a little tarp-covered shack in which you could ride out the shit storms.

She was raised in Justice, a southwest suburb of Chicago, where 294 and I-55 tangled and separated, where the late news was filled with shootings and fires and indicted politicians, where nearby forest preserves made a natural setting for drinking, drug use, freaky spiritual insights, heavy petting, and, eventually, protected and unprotected sex. At Queen of Peace High School, Sister Therese, Meg's Christian Lifestyles teacher, hung a felt banner with the heading "A Woman of Peace. . . ," under which were attributes: "feels and forgives," "cares and comforts," "respects herself and others." Meg bought into these virtues wholeheartedly, even sentimentally, though this didn't stop her from stealing beer money from her dad or getting into screaming matches with her mom or telling off someone at school who crossed her.

She ran with a crew of girls who called themselves the BBs, which stood for "best buds," "beautiful babes," and "ball busters." They smoked, swore, drank, played powder-puff football, coached each other through abortions, and when they felt like it, dolled themselves up like starlets for a night of house parties, showing their men the meaning of both dancing and fucking. Kim was their leader. She was a city kid, clever and fun and also a bossy motor-mouth who sometimes made Meg feel like dirt. Jenny was the soulful one, though not the sharpest knife in the drawer. With a huge chin that made her look like a Muppet, Patty was the friendliest, someone you could turn to when Kim was being a bitch or wanted to cut you from the group, and Colleen was the smartest and went to college.

Pure Irish on both sides, Meg herself had orange-red hair and freckles, and she cultivated an earthy, milkmaid vibe—grounded or rowdy, as the BBs needed. She had fantasized about being a farmer's wife on the Emerald Isle, living on a bluff overlooking the sea, surrounded by loving, happy children in front of a roaring fireplace. Instead, at age twenty-one she married Mark, her high school sweetheart from St. Laurence, their "brother school" across the street, honeymooned on a Caribbean cruise because he saw a discount flight advertised on a billboard on 294, and hit the marital ground running, waitressing five days a week at Pepe's Mexican restaurant on Ninety-Fifth Street.

Her children came fast and furious—at one point she had four car seats—and these kids had absolutely no sense. They gnawed on stuffed animals, crushed Froot Loops into the carpet, broke lamps and bones, spread the *Sun-Times* from room to room, climbed on her body like it was a piece of rec-room furniture, reinforced the dog's foul habits, stupefied themselves with TV and video games and computers, left pieces of clothing and plates of half-eaten food in unexpected places, and generally made everything damp and sticky and off-kilter. She threatened to shoot them, put them down the garbage disposal, hang them from a crossbeam in the garage, or drag them behind the minivan. She didn't believe in spanking, but to make a point she would come up behind Aileen or Joe or Molly or Patrick and flick a hard finger behind the ear. As a result, the kids made Bs in school, were on time to sports events, and mostly did the chores she assigned without lipping back that often—behavior that gratifyingly coincided with her main child-rearing goals.

Mark became a mechanical engineer and made decent money, but she waitressed off and on, depending. Their sex was fun and frequent though she had to draw the line on his perverted desires: blow jobs in T.G.I. Friday's parking lots were OK, but anal, no matter the venue, was not. Her favorite days were Sundays during football season, when she'd get Mark and the kids into good clothes, put on one of her classier dresses, and go to Mass with the fam. The service was boring but relaxing, unless she wanted something from God and then she would pray her ass off the whole time. At home, she would change into her Jim McMahon jersey and order pizza, and the whole family would hit the living room to watch the Bears game. She'd curl up with Mark on the stained, overstuffed leather couch (part of a living room set that had put them in a credit hole for years), yell at the refs or at the play calling of the Bears' hapless post-Ditka coaches, and get drunk. And she imagined that Mark stayed by her because he meant it, not just because the Bears were on TV.

Occasionally, she missed driving around with the BBs, getting stoned and listening to Rush and Queen and Styx, and Mark was sometimes a selfish bastard who found fault whenever possible without minding his own shit, but things basically felt stable and safe.

Then, as she liked to put it, Mark had an accident at work: he fell and his dick slipped into a coworker. During the ensuing fight, he called her fat and ugly. She called him a sad, limp prick desperate to prove his lack of manhood with every whore on two legs. She kind of thought it would blow over, actually, and wanted it to, but when Mark wasn't as apologetic as she thought he should be, she got suspicious.

"This isn't the first time," she said near the end of dinner one night. The kids were still sitting there. She should have known something was up when she had wanted to try for child number five and he'd bullied her into signing the vasectomy consent form.

Mark glared at her, no doubt mentally practicing his lines for the instant the kids would leave the table.

"I'm just never going to be good enough for you, am I?" she asked.

"No, you're not," he finally responded, right in front of the children.

"Always get witnesses," her father had said in a moment of drunken candor when she was twelve, and that's one of the things that stuck with her through the years.

She cried for weeks after Mark moved out, often crouched in her closet after putting the kids to bed. The BBs rallied around her, letting her mooch more drinks and cigarettes than usual, and her kids were better than expected. She got way involved in their emotional lives and kept them close to her. Even so, she spiraled down into what was surely a form of madness. It took her a good six months, but she finally bottomed out and said to herself that no one would ever hurt her again, she would never cry again, she would be a woman of peace.

.   .   .

As the years passed, she gained weight in all the wrong places. She felt like her own body mocked her sometimes, rearranging itself in her sleep, the way her kids used to put hats on her when she took a nap on the couch or that one time they duct-taped her wrist to the coffee table when she'd passed out during a Bears game. Sometimes her flesh embarrassed her and sometimes it made her think she was becoming something established and formidable. At Pepe's, believe it or not, there were still guys who hit on large women in their forties, scrawling first names and cell numbers on the backs of credit card receipts or giving her the eye while spanking the bottoms of their hot sauce bottles. Most men were pigs. She wasn't judging—just stating a fact.

"How's everything tasting tonight?" she asked a million times. "Anybody leave room for dessert?"

She kept in touch with the BBs, of course. Midlife was bludgeoning them all, though not equally. Kim was divorced, but she liked her job as a merchandise display director at Target and had a new boyfriend. Colleen had married a computer guy from Saudi Arabia and converted to Islam, which she found to be a great comfort. She wore a hijab and stopped drinking and smoking. Ironically, her husband wasn't all that interested in following the Koran, at least the part about women also having a say in the marriage, and he was always traveling for work or to visit family back in the Middle East, so their marriage came apart, leaving Colleen, who stayed a Muslim, to raise two kids with her accounting degree. Jenny was married to a Hickory Hills cop, had three kids, and worked on the tarmac at Midway with her noise-cancelling headphones and her red light wands, parking airplanes forty hours a week. In high school, Meg had envied Jenny's body, but she'd packed on the pounds as well.

Patty was the one who kept them all together. She never had any kids, which was sad, but her husband, a long-haul trucker, had stuck by her. She was always upbeat and a totally loyal friend. Since graduation, she'd had a sixth sense for when the BBs were drifting apart and she would organize a Sox game or a picnic in Grant Park or a girls' night out, and they were always there for each other at their kids' first communions and confirmations and graduations.

Meg also tried to put a good face on things. Her oldest, Aileen, had a job managing patient records at a dentist's office, Joe and Molly were plugging away on their associate's degrees at Daley College, and Patrick was not in prison, knock on wood. Every Monday she posted a new Irish blessing on her Facebook page: "For each petal on the shamrock this brings a wish your way. Good health, good luck, and happiness for today and every day."

.   .   .

Then Patty got super sick. The cancer started in her ovaries and spread to her liver in no time. Soon the BBs were seeing each other regularly again at Patty's house and during Patty's increasingly frequent stays at Rush Hospital. Patty said the chemo wasn't as bad as the radiation. At least she could eat mashed potatoes on chemo. The radiation was the worst—she couldn't keep anything down.

On their visits, the BBs hid their worries and reminisced to entertain Patty.

Kim said, "Remember that time Meg yelled `Bite me, Sister T!'?"

Meg laughed with everyone, but she had liked Sister Therese, who had taught her to be a woman of peace, to feel and forgive. In fact, she remembered being surprisingly happy to see Sister T emerge from the school's side entrance that Saturday afternoon, carrying a tote bag, as the BBs careened drunkenly through the parking lot in Patty's car. Meg had wanted to greet her joyously in the rough and rowdy spirit of the BBs. She stuck her whole head and shoulders out the window, and when she yelled, "Bite me, Sister T!" the nun turned, looking shocked and even scared, before she seemed to recognize Meg and a more inward look closed her face.

Meg felt guilty and then angry that what she had wanted to express came out so wrong, and she had trouble being in the same room with Sister T after that.

"She was actually nice," Meg said quietly, as if that would be the apology she could never bring herself to make. She flushed with embarrassment even after all these years.

"I loved that woman," Colleen said, nodding in her head scarf and meeting Meg's eyes earnestly, but that just made Meg feel worse.

"Then why'd you switch teams?" Kim said under her breath.

"Come on, you guys," Patty said from her hospital bed.

As if Patty's sickness were contagious, Meg developed her own health issues. After a routine gynie appointment, her doctor sent her for tests at Mercy Hospital on Twenty-Sixth Street. Something about her cervix wasn't right. Driving down to that treeless neighborhood dotted with housing project towers, in her '95 Buick Century with muffler issues, she had a feeling the day was going to suck, and she had never been more right. It sucked in every way, from her car dying, to discovering her high blood pressure and her aneurysm, to being threatened with a gun in the parking lot. But even all that didn't seem as bad as Patty being on her last legs, so the next day, when an urgent call from Kim summoned her to Patty's bedside, she hadn't told the BBs what had happened.

Patty's energy level had gotten so low she couldn't talk or swallow. She was alive but she couldn't do anything. So, while Patty's husband was out getting some food, the BBs rubbed her temples, massaged her hands, and squeezed her shoulders. They were all touching something. At one point, Jenny couldn't help saying to Patty, "You know, bub, you've been trying really hard to fight this thing, but it's time to let go." Apparently hearing these words, Patty opened her eyes for the first time in two days, looked at the four of them, closed her eyes, and passed, just like that.

.　　.　　.

At the wake, they had a buffet with sandwiches and fruit and veggie platters, a slide show, and pictures on poster board. Up in the front were the casket and flowers. The BBs ordered an enormous floral arrangement in the shape of a flamingo with a sign that said, "BBs Forever." Kim was really proud of it. "Meg, Meg," she said, "look up there. Which one do you think is ours?" She knew Kim was fishing, so she said, "Great job, Kim." Walking to the front of that room and seeing Patty lying in the casket like a dummy in a wax museum, her face reinflated and coated with makeup, was one of the hardest things Meg had ever done.

Afterward, everyone wanted to drink. Usually Colleen wouldn't go out with them because apparently even going to a bar without drinking was haram (a sin), but tonight she said it was more important to be together. For Meg, religion and drinking went hand in glove, but she always tried to be respectful of her friend's strange beliefs. The BBs were joined by Steve, who was Kim's new boyfriend, and Laura, a friend of Patty's who had gone to their high school but wasn't a BB. Laura lived in Minneapolis and was going to sing at the funeral the next day.

They ended up at a really nice Italian restaurant in a strip mall on 110th Street with outdoor seating facing the parking lot. They sat outside so people could smoke. It was getting dark by now. The patio was enclosed with black railings and lit with old-style street lamps.

Kim sat at the head of the table, holding court with her cigarette up in the air. She wore her hair dyed and feathered exactly as it had been in the late '70s, her eyebrows slightly darker. She'd poured herself into a tight skirt with a slit on the side, some of her overflowing into a muffin top, noticeable through her satin blouse. Steve sat at the other end of the table from Kim. He was a small guy but in good shape, with short hair pointed like an arrow down his forehead and a trimmed beard. Jenny took out a four-by-six photo of Patty, standing alone on her wedding day, and propped it against a condiment caddy, facing toward the center of the table.

While their waiter, Frankie, was trying to recite the specials, Kim said to him, "Lose the bow tie—it makes you look like a six-year-old."

Frankie stared back at her. Meg had dealt with many asshole customers herself, but she laughed. As long as Kim was aimed elsewhere, Meg could deal with her.

"We're just drinking," Kim added, like she was breaking a spell. "Who wants to split a bucket of beers with me?"

They hadn't met Steve before, so once they placed their orders Laura began asking him a lot of questions.

"Steve is great," Kim butted in. "As you all know, I have zero bladder capacity. I have to pee constantly. I even peed on Steve. Steve is like, 'No big deal.' That's why I love him."

"You're robbing the cradle," Colleen said. Most of them knew Steve was about ten years younger than Kim, and Kim was proud of it.

"Anyone from eighteen to eighty," Steve said. "Eighteen to eighty. That's my motto."

Kim said, "I told Steve, `If you don't like my friends, you don't like me.'"

"You are so right, Kim," Jenny said.

When Frankie brought them their drinks, Kim said, "Thanks, Frankie. But do me a favor—lose the pants, too."

Kim laughed at her own joke, and Meg saw how it could be funny, but she was starting to wish Kim would lay off.

"Hey, everybody, listen up," Kim said. She raised her beer bottle. "I just want to say something. Guys, we lost a great friend and it sucks. When Patty got sick, I didn't think I could ever say something like this, but it was great to be with her at the end. I felt very peaceful when she passed. All my anxiety went away. I had a very, very strong feeling of peace. I think that says something about the kind of person Patty was. She was fucking awesome. To Patty!"

"To Patty!" everyone said, and everyone drank.

Meg herself had been surprised by what an incredible experience Patty's last moments had been. "Yeah," she said, "it was so moving. I—"

"Hey!" Kim shouted down the table, jabbing her cigarette at Steve. "You're paying for all this! You got that?"

Steve nodded, pursing his lips in a funny way.

"Guys, guys! Steve is paying tonight, so knock yourselves out."

Everybody did knock themselves out, pounding drinks until they got the munchies, just like old times, so Kim flagged down Frankie and they ordered some pizzas.

"I don't know about those doctors," Jenny said while everyone was stuffing themselves. "Nothing they ever did seemed to slow the cancer down. I just don't understand why they couldn't have helped Patty more."

"That's because you're not as bright as the other girls," Kim said, and she winked at Jenny. "That's what the guidance counselor said in high school," Kim explained to the rest of the table. "Remember that? He said Jenny wasn't college material, that asshole."

Kim herself had gone to a tiny college in Indiana that didn't even have a football team. Colleen went to DePaul, but you never heard her lord her college over anyone. Meg wanted to stick up for Jenny, but she didn't know the right words. Kim was always telling that story, supposedly to call out the mean guidance counselor, but now Jenny was staring into the parking lot, probably looking for a place to hide, the way Meg had felt when Kim brought up Sister T at Patty's bedside.

There were times over the years when Meg felt that Kim was simply the collective voice of the BBs, channeling all of the group's wisdom and rough humor. In fact, it had been Kim who one night described Mark as having an accident at work where he fell and his dick slipped into a coworker. At first, Meg hadn't been comfortable hearing Kim blab details of her marriage going down the toilet, but Meg had taken up the expression herself. It consoled her in a way she couldn't explain.

But now Meg felt barraged by Kim's endless words, as if no one else had anything to say. Patty could put Kim in her place, nicely, if necessary, and Meg missed her horribly right now. She was even missing Mark, that selfish cheating prick. She could feel a weepy drunk coming on, and she hated those. It was hard to be a woman of peace during a shit storm. She bummed a cigarette from Jenny, even though because of her aneurysm the doctor had said, "Quit immediately and forever." What if she keeled over right here? It wouldn't be pretty. She lit up, took a drag, ashed onto the patio's stone tiles.

Before Kim could take over the conversation again, Meg said to Colleen, "You know, I haven't shaved in weeks. I was kind of worried about it, but my hair grows in blonde and you can't really see it. All of my body hair is really soft."

"Can I touch it?" Laura asked, poising a finger above Meg's forearm.

Everyone laughed at this. The BBs had always talked about their body hair back in the day. They were always letting their pits grow and having hairiest legs contests, unless a huge date was coming up.

Meg swallowed the last of her beer, and, just as Kim had been doing, she crammed the bottle, neck first, back into the ice bucket, then took another. Kim rattled on like a jackhammer, telling another story about her job at Target. Each story was the same: Kim had an idea, some dumb ass contradicted it, Kim went ahead anyway, and the display was a huge success. "I always get what I want," Kim said, and she glared down the table at Steve. "Remember that." Steve also worked at Target, though Meg couldn't figure out what he did, and he vouched for everything Kim said.

When Meg had smoked her cigarette all the way down, she bummed another one from Jenny. She didn't give a fuck. She would smoke until her aneurysm exploded right here, and she would die in front of the BBs, and they would all feel bad about her passing like they felt bad for Patty, and that would be something. Maybe that would get Kim to shut up for five seconds. But right now the thought of her own useless death was just about enough to make Meg cry, and, fuck it, she wasn't going to start crying for no apparent reason in front of everybody the night of Patty's wake.

"You guys are never going to believe what happened to me," she boomed in her loudest voice.

"What?" Jenny said.

Kim kept talking about her work heroics.

"I got attacked at gunpoint in the Mercy Hospital parking lot."

"Really?" Laura said.

"Worst day of my life, worst day ever. Listen, listen, listen, you guys," Meg said loudly, and Kim finally stopped talking.

"OK," Meg said in a quieter tone. "So I go in for my gynie last month—Steve, you're going to have to bear with me here—and the doc says there's something with my cervix, a growth there that maybe isn't right, and he wants me to go to Mercy for some tests, and this and that. Not really feeling like a trip to the hood, but it's doctor's orders, right? So I drive down there, and my car fucking stalls out in the parking lot. I'm already late for my appointment and I have to literally push my car into a spot to keep from blocking people in. Then I realize I've locked everything in the car—my keys, my purse, my phone—everything. So I'm already, like, this is the worst day ever.

"So, anyway, I run to the doctor's office, and the receptionist goes, 'Well, your appointment, blah, blah, blah,' and I'm like, 'Don't. Do not even start with me,' but I don't say anything. Get in there, turns out my blood pressure is two hundred eight over a hundred."

"This is serious," Steve said, as if he knew about medical facts.

"My God, Meg, you were so stressed," Jenny said.

"Jenny, it was more than stress, I swear. The doctor says, 'You can't leave the hospital. We cannot let you leave with that blood pressure.' They put me on an IV to lower it, and then they did an MRI and found I have an aneurysm in my brain."

"Oh no," Colleen said.

"And they can't even operate or take it out because of where it is. My artery has a huge balloon on it that could blow at any time."

Meg paused to let this sink in. She put out the cigarette that was smoldering between her fingers, looked at the congealing remnants of pepperoni pizza on her plate, glanced at her beer—everything the doctor had told her not to do with that constipated look on his face. But Patty was dead, and she couldn't be expected to follow such strict instructions today.

"It would be a huge stroke," Meg added, in case people weren't getting the picture. "I could die just like that."

"Don't say that," Jenny said solemnly, looking directly at her.

Kim was staring at something on the table. Her burning cigarette sent up smoke like the chimney of a tiny factory.

"So, now, I'm thinking, great, things can't get any worse," Meg continued. "I've got a fucking time bomb in my head. They finally let me leave and it's like four in the afternoon, and all I've had is breakfast and I'm absolutely starving. So I call my mom, and my brother's going to come over as soon as he gets off work to break into the car and give me a jump, and I go out to the parking lot to wait for my brother, and I'm standing by my car when this guy starts coming toward me through the lot. He goes, 'Ma'am, ma'am, excuse me.'"

"Black guy?" Kim asked.

"Yeah, he was black," Meg said, looking hard at Kim. "But that's not the point."

Nodding, Laura asked, "What happened?"

Kim picked a fleck of something off her lip, inspected it, wiped it on a napkin.

"Anyway," Meg said, "he goes, 'Ma'am, excuse me, can you help me? Can I ask you something?' and I'm waving my arms at him. I'm like, 'No, no. I don't have anything, I don't know anything,' but he kept coming at me, and I kept waving him off, and then, when he's about five feet away, he pulls out a gun and says if I don't give him all my cash he's going to shoot me."

"Oh my god," Colleen said quietly.

Meg was now reliving those moments in every detail. The guy had been more compact than large—Meg probably outweighed him—and he wore a long bright-yellow T-shirt as big as a dress. There was a blue padlock design on the center of the T-shirt and the padlock was open. The legs of the man's dark shorts were stiff and wide and went to midcalf. His eyes were flat and excited at the same time. His brown face was glistening with sweat. His mouth seemed ready to smile, as if this was all a joke, but he never so much as smirked.

"And that was it," Meg said. "I just fucking lost it. I go, 'Then you're going to have to shoot me, all right? Because my purse is locked in the car, and my friend's dying, and I've got an aneurysm in my brain, and you're just going to have to fucking shoot me! Go ahead, shoot me! Shoot me!!'"

Meg noticed she was now shouting across the patio of the restaurant. In fact, she had also told the man that her husband had cheated on her—she had needed to tell him everything if she was going to end up dying in a parking lot—but she didn't include that part now.

"I was screaming at him to shoot me," she boomed. "I didn't care if my aneurysm blew. I was so hungry and pissed off I almost passed out. And he looked me in the eye, and he went like this"—she imitated his nod—"because he got it, he fucking got it, he heard what I was saying, and he put his gun back in his waistband, pulled his shirt over it, and kept walking."

"Holy shit," Jenny said.

"Good for you," Laura said.

"He thought he had you," Steve said. "But you had him."

Kim took a long, silent drag on her cigarette and spouted smoke high into the air, like a breaching whale, making meaningful eye contact with Steve.

Meg nodded once, hard, to agree with what everyone had said. She couldn't say anything else just then, which was more than OK because, for the moment, it felt as if she'd never need to speak again.

Suddenly everyone's attention was overwhelming, especially Colleen's, and Meg looked around the patio. The place had emptied out except for their table. She noticed Frankie slipping through the door back into the restaurant. She hadn't been aware of him while she told her story, but she hoped he had listened. Then into the silence, she heard herself say with a laugh, "Somebody give me a cigarette. I've got to calm down."

"Holy shit is right, Meg," Kim said, and she handed Meg one of her Kools.

"Can you fucking believe that?" Meg asked everyone, getting her lighter out of her purse. "Unbelievable. I didn't want to say anything because of Patty, but I had to tell you guys because you're my best buds."

"BBs forever," Jenny said.

But without Patty, Meg wondered whether the BBs would remain best buds for as long as she would remember the hold-up man's nod. She imagined the man sitting around with his own friends, telling the story of what had happened between them. "Then this white bitch went ape shit," she heard him say, and this almost made her smile.

Meg put the cigarette Kim had given her into the corner of her mouth. Getting Kim to cough up a cigarette was a victory, no doubt, but sometimes she hated Kim—she had to admit it—just as she had come to hate Mark. She knew Sister T would say that's not how a woman of peace was supposed to feel and forgive, but people had better fucking respect her. That was the most important thing.

"BBs forever," Meg repeated.

Then she lit up, as if that were the same as raising a toast, and took an enormous drag on the cigarette, filling her chest, and even, she imagined, sending smoke to her aneurysm, until it seemed that both her chest and her head would burst. As she exhaled, she caught a look of concern on Colleen's face, as if she didn't get that Meg had made her worst day into her best day. But she was done explaining herself. She quickly took another puff and refused to knock from her cigarette the glowing piece of trembling gray ash.

My Nonsexual Affair

A Tale of Strong and Unusual Feelings

My nonsexual affair began on the day Linda and I had hot-fudge sundaes, in the park, near the fence, where most of the grass was dead and the weeds could not be identified by anyone who was not a trained botanist.

Luckily, Linda was.

"*Ambrosia artemisiifolia*," she said. "See the hairy underside of the leaf? Ragweed, people call it. Bad for allergies."

"Fascinating," I said.

She smiled to herself in a way I found mysterious. Her fingertips lingered on the underside of the weed's leaves as she released it, a gesture both sensual and vaguely scientific.

I had never known anyone who could call a weed by its true name. I wanted to hold her brain in my bare hands.

"It doesn't get any better than this!" I exclaimed. In my excitement, I bit the inside of my lip. I soon tasted blood, but this was the most enthusiasm I'd felt in years.

Linda straightened up yet continued to examine the nearby

plants with her hands on her hips. "How's work?" she finally asked, turning back to me.

I tongued my wound before answering. "For some reason, I had 'Rhinestone Cowboy' playing in my head all day."

"Glen Campbell?"

"Yeah," I said. "'Gettin' cards and letters from people I don't even know.'"

"'And offers comin' over the phone.'"

My breath caught slightly as I realized she'd completed the lyric for me.

"Linda," I said.

"What?"

"Nothing."

"No, I'm listening. Let me know what you're thinking." She tilted her head and squinted in her trademark quizzical expression. To an almost violent degree, she invited me to reveal a confidence.

"Well, sometimes I wonder if we've gotten to know each other —a little *too* well."

"Oh, don't be ridiculous," she said. "You're a puzzle to me. I definitely don't understand you."

"You and my wife both," I said, and immediately regretted it. It had been an unspoken rule to mention our partners as little as possible.

Linda had been sitting with her knees pulled up and her forearms wrapped around her knees, but now she extended her right leg and her right hand fell to her thigh, while she kept her left forearm around her left kneecap. I knew this meant she was extremely upset.

"Kidding," I said.

"I bet."

"Kidding," I said again, more earnestly.

"All right, you clodhopper," she said, and pushed my shoulder. I swayed as if she had sent me moving like a tire swing. She didn't seem to notice.

"Good ice cream," she said. "Gotta get back." She stood up and brushed off her knees, though they were already clean.

We ambled over to a green trash barrel that smelled rancid from five paces. We tossed in our plastic sundae boats and spoons and napkins, then veered toward the street where our cars were parked a block apart.

"Wow, that was fun," I said.

"It sure was. Hey," she said, stopping and making intense eye contact. "You take care?"

"No, *you* take care."

"Get out of here!" she said.

As she walked away, I asked, "You watching *Lost* this week?"

"Of course. Facebook chat?"

"Maybe." I winked.

"Sheesh!" she said, waving her hand at me. But she was smiling.

.　　.　　.

When I got home, Sarah had the lawn mower all taken to pieces in the garage. I left the Camry in the driveway and walked up to her with my hands in my pockets, whistling.

"Jesus Christ," Sarah said, "is that chocolate sauce down the front of your shirt?"

I looked down. Sure enough, there was a long streak of fudge sauce, slightly thicker where it crossed the bulge of my paunch.

I blushed. Why hadn't Linda said something?

"Where?" I asked, on the brink of spilling a confession. "Oh, *that*," I said, dabbing at the sauce with a finger. My mind flashed again, almost angrily, to Linda. "You know, I got a lot done, so I stopped for a sundae on my way home. It's bizarre that something can get on you without you even noticing!" In fact, I had no memory of dribbling anything. Was it blood from my lip? I touched my finger to my tongue. Fudge sauce. I tried to laugh and finally looked up to risk Sarah's gaze, but she was rummaging in her toolbox as if I weren't even there.

When I got inside, in the home Sarah and I had made together with our nine-year-old daughter, Joslyn, I had a flash of guilt: Is this how it's going to be from now on? Sneaking around? Lying? The sauce made me feel unclean in more ways than one. But that would be what someone having a sexual affair would think, and there was *nothing sexual* happening with Linda. We had found a special kind of friendship, that was all.

"This shirt's a mess!" I exclaimed loudly in the mudroom, hoping my voice would carry into the garage. I removed the shirt, doused it with Spray 'n Wash, and rinsed it in the utility sink.

.   .   .

Things had begun innocently enough.

The campus where Linda taught was close to the downtown bank where I worked. There was a café, frequented mostly by students, which sold fantastic sandwich wraps. One day our orders came up right at the same time, and we realized we had both purchased the same kind of wrap—spicy Thai chicken! It turned out that we also shared a love for the sun on a warm day. "Great minds think alike," I said, as we settled within speaking distance on a pair of benches outside the café. I was referring to our common choice of sandwich, but I also could have been referring to our affinity for alfresco dining, which would become a theme in our relationship. "So I see you like your spicy Thai wrap with a little photosynthesis on the side," I added, nodding up at the sun.

This was how I learned she was a trained botanist.

And just like that, a bond had formed, and we continued to run into each other at the café, sort of randomly, until it started to seem intentional. We had become friends. "You enjoy talking about things in a way others don't" was how Linda put it one day. I reminded her that I was a CPA, more comfortable with FASB regulations than deep conversation. And when she pshawed that, I told her I'd been a jock, too, back in the day. She looked at me with what I would come to recognize as her quizzical expression, as if she thought I was referring to myself as an actual jockstrap and not as an athlete. I clarified for her that I had played collegiate soccer. "Albeit Division Three," I added modestly. Her laugh was easy and, I thought, musical. Unlike Sarah, she never wore makeup, and that felt like a sort of guiding principle for us.

So we were good random friends, you could say. Casual friends—until today, when we had *planned* to meet on an otherwise ho-hum Sunday afternoon, under the pretext of "catching up on things" at work. And she had named that weed, and we had crossed a line.

.   .   .

Two weeks later, in early June, Linda and I were walking through a stretch of forest in Saugatuck Dunes State Park, heading for the beach. Sarah had taken Joslyn to pick up her new mouth guard and to shop for leotards for her dance class.

"I think I'll go to a wooded area and journal," I'd told Sarah.

"Bring me back some nuts and berries," she had said. "But could you do some dishes before you go, babe?"

Babe was a term of endearment from early in our relationship. Sarah first used the term while affectionately slapping me on the buttocks after we'd had intercourse in the shower in my dormitory at three in the morning. Sarah played volleyball at the Midwestern liberal arts college where I played soccer. We relished sexual contact early in our relationship to an almost compulsive degree. Every athlete has a teammate with whom there's an unusual level of intuitive connection—passes always connect, the ball arcs perfectly to set up the spike. Sarah and I had had that connection in bed. It was the foundation upon which we had built our love, eighteen years ago. But as our marriage progressed, it seemed as if we were competing with our old selves or maybe even with each other. Our couplings sometimes felt like tests of endurance or a type of exercise drill. Occasionally, one of us would make anguished cries in the middle of sex, like a weight lifter.

Soon I'd done all the dishes, my teeth just about chattering from nervousness. It took all of my self-discipline to wipe down the cutting boards as well; I didn't want Sarah to have any reason to think that I'd rushed to get to the state park for something other than journaling.

"What's your biggest fear?" Linda asked me now, as we strolled on the path through the woods.

"You really know how to cut through all the BS," I said admiringly.

"Just answer the question."

"That I'll love too much," I said. "Or not enough." I glanced over at her. Her gaze moved among the many species of flora that surrounded us.

"Look at that," she said. "*Arisaema triphyllum*. A jack-in-the-pulpit." Just off the trail, she knelt down by a small green plant with a few lance-shaped leaves illuminated by sunshine dappling through the trees above. Her shoulder-length brown hair fell forward and I saw a part of her slender neck I had never seen before. She pushed back a green, overarching hood to reveal an upright flower spike. "He's pretty proud of himself," she said.

My throat became too thick for me to speak.

We walked on another hundred yards, going up the last rise before the trail sloped toward the edge of the woods and the water beyond.

"What's *your* biggest fear?" I asked.

She laughed at this, then beamed to herself in a strange, self-satisfied way.

"That I'll end up somewhere I don't want to be," she finally said.

It was hard to parse her tone. Her partner, Miklosh, was an economics professor at Hope College, where Linda also taught. He frequently wrote letters to the editor of *The Holland Sentinel* bemoaning the dangers of fiat currency and advocating a return to the gold standard.

We broke through the trees and found ourselves on top of a dune overlooking Lake Michigan.

"Hey, those waves are like wrinkles on a huge forehead," I observed, feeling inspired.

"Last one in is a rotten egg!" Linda cried, and we took off.

The dune sloped down gently, but the sand was extremely soft and deep, so my feet sank into it, making it hard to run quickly. But I ran as fast as I could toward the water. I tried to take off my shoes while running—to complete the effect of running down the dune and into the water—but I couldn't and had to stop to remove my shoes. Linda caught up to me, breathing hard, and passed me. Still, it was great.

And the day went from there. We told each other difficult stories about our families of origin—how my father had once thrown a pumpkin at me in anger, how he once doubted whether I had the brains or the fortitude to become a CPA. Linda told me of the time her mother cracked a raw egg over her head because she wasn't paying attention while her mother was trying to teach her a recipe. We both admitted that we'd been thinking of each other as a "new dimension" in our lives—the exact same phrase!

"No, let me prove it to you," I exclaimed. "Let me show you my journal!"

But she told me she didn't need to read it in my journal. She trusted me.

.   .   .

Things had gone so well that when we made it back to the parking lot, I was tempted, because I felt we could handle it now, to bring up the fudge sauce on my shirt that fateful day and ask Linda why she'd never said anything about it. "I don't want to judge you," I had practiced saying, "but that seems like the sort of thing a friend would tell a friend." Instead, I said, very frankly, "I felt amazingly close to you today."

"You did," she said. She smiled, but her tone had a certain careful quality to it.

"Yeah, so close that I didn't want to tell you *how* close while we were walking along the beach."

She said nothing, looked at me blankly.

"What am I doing?" I exclaimed. "I'm sorry, this is uncharted territory for me!" My sense of our surroundings seemed to spin 360 degrees.

"What are you trying to say?" Linda asked. "I've never seen you so emotional."

"High on life? I don't know. Hey, some ice cream? I'm in the mood."

That quizzical look was back, but all at once it broke, and she smiled hugely. "You know what? You're nuts! You're just a really unique person." Then she lowered her eyes, as if now she was the one who had gone too far.

"Hey, it's all right," I said. "You know? We can *talk* to each other. What the heck!"

The truth of this seemed to dawn slowly on her. "Yeah, what the heck," she said and renewed her smile.

.   .   .

When I got home that afternoon, Sarah was just coming upstairs from the basement, where we had an elliptical trainer, an exercise bike, and a weight station. She was drenched in sweat. Her face was flushed and her reddish-brown hair was pulled back in a ponytail. She toed off her shoes in the mudroom, and then in a single fluid motion, slipped off her sweaty gym shorts and panties and draped them over the laundry hamper. She was high-waisted, softly muscular, and nearly as tall as me.

"Joslyn's at Lindsey's," she said, stepping by me and heading down the hallway. "Get yourself ready."

I used the first-floor shower and she used the larger shower on the second floor. We met in our bedroom and engaged in a wild, heaving sexual act, repeatedly switching positions so that she was on top for a while and then I was on top. Either way, what we were doing reminded me of a bull trying to buck its rider. Still, we persevered until we both came.

After we were finished, I lay on my back and closed my eyes, imagining wave after Lake Michigan wave breaking along a sandy beach.

"You're a total mystery to me," I murmured, and then I drifted off to sleep.

.   .   .

Then one afternoon, I got an urgent phone call from Linda. "I've got to get out of here," she said. "Let's meet at the state park." I was behind schedule on some regulatory filings, but they could wait.

As was our custom, we parked our cars at different ends of the lot and converged at the trailhead as if we were both just coincidentally headed for a solitary hike. And in fact we barely spoke to each other until we were on the beach, sitting on the warm sand, watching the waves come in.

Apparently, politics in the Biology Department at the college were rough. Linda felt disrespected by several things that had been said in a meeting and then alluded to in an e-mail that went out to the whole division. I was so focused on being there for her, I had trouble following everything she said, but I definitely understood the tears she had to wipe from her eyes.

I wanted to put my arm around her, but I knew how embraces sometimes lead to sex. Yet I knew our affair was nonsexual, so my embrace would be innocent. But I also feared that, emotionally, I was cheating on my wife already, so none of this was innocent. Finally, I patted her knee and said, "I'm so sorry this is happening to you."

"Thanks for listening," she said. She patted my knee right back. "Miklosh is to the point where he just rolls his eyes when I complain about those people."

Despite the fact that now she, too, had broken our implicit pact not to mention our partners, I had never felt so close to Linda. To be honest, I wanted to do more than pat her knee. I wanted a gesture that would speak the new, intense, but nonsexual language we were learning.

When I got back to the office, I tried to make progress on those regulatory filings, but my feelings were rising and coalescing and falling in unpredictable ways, like the contents of a lava lamp. Finally, I decided I needed to journal to settle down. My thoughts were awkward and confused, until I wrote: *Is it possible to have* EMOTIONAL INTERCOURSE?

.　　.　　.

That evening during family-workout time in the basement, I became engrossed in a CNN segment on the aftermath of the battle between Israel and Hamas. The senseless conflict reminded me of Linda's difficulties in her Biology Department. Joslyn was practicing new moves for her modern-dance class in front of a floor-to-ceiling mirror, I was taking it easy on the exercise bike, watching the TV, and when Sarah finished on the elliptical, she said something I didn't catch and went upstairs.

Fifteen minutes later, she came back down to the basement showered but red faced, wearing her bathrobe with the belt knotted extremely tightly across her waist.

"Where is your head at?" she asked in a low, tense voice. Joslyn was practicing a vaulting leap just a few steps away, and I hoped she hadn't overheard. Then Sarah turned and left.

At first I thought she was scolding me for easing up on my workout again. She had noted on other occasions that despite exercising regularly I had reached a point where I consumed more calories than I burned. I followed her upstairs, all the way to our bedroom on the second floor. It turned out she was angry that I had not picked up on her cue to finish my workout, shower, and prepare for sex, which we could still accomplish with some assurance of privacy as long as Joslyn was absorbed with perfecting her dance routine.

"I'm sorry, Sarah," I said, "but I was watching this special report on the Israel-Hamas conflict."

Sarah sighed and let me use the upstairs shower. While I lathered up, she sat on the toilet lid and asked me about my day.

"Nothing special," I said, grateful that the sound of water spraying would conceal any awkwardness. "Working on those regulatory filings. How about you?"

"Everything's peachy," she said. "I got some reports to run and made some users happy." Sarah was a computer programmer who faced constant struggles with the clients who relied on her work. "We're all right," she added, maybe trying to make up with me. "Joslyn has over twenty minutes of her workout left."

Still, our sex was lackluster.

I had trouble sleeping that night and slipped out of bed to journal. *Something going on with Sarah and me,* I wrote. *Is Linda the problem or the solution or...????*

. . .

A few evenings later, I told Sarah I was going back to work for a bit, but instead I went to Linda's house uninvited. I had two reusable green grocery bags full of things—food, a book, a few DVDs. I felt ready for whatever might happen.

"Hi, it's me," I said, when Linda answered the door. "Allan, what are you doing here?"

"Just stopping by. Just hanging out, I guess."

"Miklosh is here," she said, with significance in her voice.

"That's fine. Does he want to hang out as well?"

"Who is it?" Miklosh said, coming to the door.

Linda's partner was a small man, maybe fifteen years older than Linda. I don't wish to criticize anyone's appearance, but Miklosh was not what is commonly considered handsome or even average. Linda was pretty, with her bright eyes and pert chin, but she was beyond any superficial concern with appearances.

"I'm a friend of Linda's," I said. I blushed hotly. At this point I knew I had made a horrible mistake, and yet a part of me insisted that what I was doing was OK, that the awkwardness I felt was a necessary consequence of personal growth, which was always uncomfortable. "I was in the neighborhood, so I just dropped by to see if you guys wanted to hang out. I brought some bagels, some cherries, and some chips and salsa, plus some DVDs—*Slumdog Millionaire* and the third season of *The Office,* the American version. What are you guys up to?"

Linda's expression suggested that she had just tasted spoiled food. "Hey, wow, Allan, thanks for stopping by," she managed. "This is great stuff. But we're busy tonight. Sorry!"

"No problem," I said.

Walking back to my car, I wondered what I had been thinking. Had I been recklessly insisting on our innocence or madly expressing our guilt? I admit I was not entirely myself.

When I returned home, Sarah confronted me in the kitchen. "You go shopping?" she asked, gesturing at the grocery bags.

There was something about her tone. I didn't have the energy to explain myself, to lie, to do anything. There were a million ways out of the situation, but it was as if I wanted to get caught.

"What's wrong?" Sarah asked, drawn further into suspicion, no doubt, by my stymied expression.

"I was at a friend's." It was only after I said this that I remembered I had told her I was going back to work.

"Who's that?"

"Miklosh," I said.

"Miklosh?"

"Yes, he teaches at the college."

"And then you went shopping?"

"Yes. And I picked up some DVDs."

.   .   .

Later that night, in bed, it seemed that something was troubling Sarah.

"What's up?" I asked, lying next to her.

She stared at the ceiling. Her mouth was sullen.

"We're a total mismatch, Allan," she said softly. "I don't love you anymore."

"What are you talking about?"

But all of a sudden I knew that my worst fear had come true: I was in a loveless marriage. She bit her lip and wouldn't answer.

"It's my fault," I said. "I haven't been giving enough to us. I've been distracted, sort of. Can you feel it?"

"I am such an idiot," Sarah said to herself. "Blind as a fucking bat."

.   .   .

Sarah withdrew from me, but she didn't leave. After a few days, she said we should try counseling. I agreed but was worried that our sessions would inevitably lead me to confess my nonsexual affair.

Maybe Sarah was right. Maybe we were mismatched after all. I suppose someone observing our marriage might say Sarah was rough on me, that her manner with me had evolved to the point where she was more like a domineering coach than a trusted teammate, but I knew that all of the real love she had ever experienced in her life before we met was from hard-ass coaches. We are all doomed to love the way we're taught to love. And who was I to criticize her? I was having an affair. I had put my family unit in jeopardy, yet I still couldn't deny myself the heady draught of intense friendship that was tearing my life apart. Though Linda had forgiven my surprise visit to her house, I had to know where I stood with her—at any cost.

. . .

"I guess the word *special* is overused," I said to Linda. "It's just that I feel the need to, I don't know, *consecrate* what we're doing."

She gave me that quizzical look. "Where are you going with this, Allan?"

We were at the beach again, both of us playing hooky, midweek. There was no point sitting at my desk—I didn't know a credit from a debit, a receivable from a payable. A few dozen yards away, another couple stretched out reading on their towels, and there were a few scattered families closer to the water, but otherwise the beach was fairly empty on this cool, overcast day.

"I got you this." From my shirt pocket I pulled out a simple silver band, very thin, and held it in my palm. She could put it on any finger and no one would know what it meant.

"Allan?"

"It's a friendship ring."

"Oh."

"I've been doing a lot of thinking," I said. "Things aren't great at home right now, and it's made me really think about everything, everything that's been going on, and why people need to be with other people, and what does it all mean, you know? No one understands what we're doing. But I believe in what we have, and I want to know how much you believe in it. Are we *friends*?"

"Of course we are, you clodhopper," she said, trying to affect our old camaraderie, but her face was showing signs of distress.

"Then accept this special ring from me."

"Well, all right."

"Go ahead, put it on."

She picked it out of my palm. She put it on the index finger of her right hand. "Ta-da," she said, trying to make light of it. "It's cool. Thanks, Allan."

"And now, with the ring on your hand, I'd like us to do something to consecrate and prove what we have. It may sound a little weird, but bear with me."

"All right." She winced slightly, but unmistakably, yet I knew I had to go through with it.

"I'd like us to sit here together on this beautiful beach and sort of, well, through our clothes, cup each other's genitals with one hand—but wait, wait, it won't be anything sexual. I want us to do it like a handshake, like something that signifies how we're not sexual at all. It'll be honoring what we have with our partners and honoring what *we* have together. Can you do that with me, right now?"

"Allan . . ." Her lower lip trembled. "Allan, I don't know what to say."

I couldn't bear to look at her. My eyes went to the water. The nearby couple had gotten up from their towels and decided to brave the chilly lake. They were stepping tentatively into the ankle-deep surf.

"You don't have to speak," I said.

"Allan, I'm sorry but you're freaking me out right now."

A prickly, cold sensation crawled up my spine. When the waves began to break a few yards out, they made rippling, splashing sounds, like distant applause; then when they reached the shore they pounded a roar of deeper notes, like something happening underground.

"You've never been committed like I have," I said quietly. I heard the bitterness in my voice, and I knew my weaker nature had temporarily assumed the upper hand, but there was nothing I could do to stop it. "This has all been just a game to you. A lark."

"That's not fair, Allan. That's mean!" She was about to cry.

"Well then, what about the time I had chocolate sauce down my front and you didn't say anything?"

"What?"

"When we had the sundaes in the park!"

"What does that matter?"

"Did you even notice?"

"Well, yeah, I guess I did."

"Then why didn't you say something?"

Tears spilled down her face. "I don't know," she said. "I don't know." She was really thinking. Finally she said, "Because I didn't know how to tell you what was happening! I didn't know what *was* happening!"

With this, she got up and strode away. I watched her all the way up the dune, until she disappeared into the woods. I didn't know how to go after her, in that moment.

I turned back to the lake. The couple had been making progress, wading in water up to their crotches. Then, suddenly, at some signal between the two of them—maybe a count?—they dove in at the same time. When they surfaced, he flipped his hair expertly to the side, flinging droplets. She pulled up on the straps of her bikini top and cried out at the coldness of the water. He said something to her.

She laughed, but then replied, "No, you didn't!" and splashed him.

Which surprised me.

.　　.　　.

Sarah and I are still together. Counseling has been good for us, or at least it's kept everything from coming completely apart. We've talked about the coach-player dynamic. We've talked about friend-ship within marriage. "Why is everything so goddamn lonely all the time?" Sarah asked the other day. And neither the therapist nor I ventured an answer. Honestly, I sit on the couch with her once a week because I'm afraid she *will* leave me, or she won't and we'll still hurt Joslyn in some subtle way we won't ever be able to understand, much less heal.

I've never confessed to Sarah the nonsexual affair, in therapy or in any other context. And though I know how dangerous and destructive my affair proved to be, a crazy question will sometimes occur to me out of the blue: Should Linda and I have done more to express our love? Should we have gone sexual? There is a natural progression to things, which, you could say, we resisted, but I believe our adventure was singular, and as a result it is something to be cherished. Now when I see Linda on the sidewalk or at a conve-nience store (never at our café, which I still frequent), I nod at her and say a solemn hello. She ignores me, of course, but so thoroughly that I can't forget how much we once meant to each other.

Windows Reflect Some Light

I.

He was placing the sprinkler on his small front lawn when she got out of her two-tone Buick Le Sabre at the curb and approached. "It's me," she said.

She went right by him, up his porch steps, and into his house, while he stood on the lawn.

He had never seen her before.

Through a window, he caught glimpses of her indistinct form, like a fish in turbid water. He stepped toward the window, its glass both reflecting light and letting it through. Then he leaned down, and through the bottom open half of the old double-hung window, he said: "I don't believe we've met."

"I am who I said I was," she replied, "and that's all that matters." She threw her handbag and a thick, three-ring binder on his dining room table.

He laughed to himself. He pressed three fingers against the

window screen. "I don't think you're likely to be the type of person I can expect you to be."

"And isn't that kind of exciting?" she called back.

It did intrigue him that she had gone into his house ahead of him, as if she had a prior claim or was at least fantastically rude, a disposition which he thought had a lot of potential somehow.

He decided it was time to go into his house.

"And if I crawl across your living room floor on my hands and knees like a naughty maid, would you spank me?" she asked, as he stepped inside.

"Pardon?"

"I said, are you interested in new shades for all these bare windows? That's what I sell." She stood hipshot near a dining room chair.

"You sell shades?" He might have misheard her the first time or he might have heard her perfectly.

He looked closely at her, as if he had never seen a person before. Her face had a pleasing bilateral symmetry. Since everyone he had ever known had refused to die, the world had taken on the sameness of a painting hung over a couch in a living room for decades, impervious to the change of seasons and all the different shades of light.

Why, he wondered, why had no one close to him fallen off a cliff or been hit by a car so as to give his life that spark of drama that made watching TV shows after a long day somehow more poignant? Why did he seem to live in an emotional eddy of some kind?

He was young. He wasn't sure.

He was surfing his first full-time job: writing trust operations software for a midsize regional bank. Some might have said he had bought more home than he could afford, but he knew better. He would not rent.

"I sell window coverings of all kinds—drapes, blinds, shades," she said, walking past him and into the living room. "Burnt-orange drapes would suit your windows there. The ones in front. The painting over the mantel has to go."

"I know," he said.

II.

They had three children, each arriving like lightning striking the same golf putter raised in triumph three separate times. It had been a long while since the curves of her body had excited him. She sometimes wore windbreakers indoors now.

Then one afternoon, after he had poured Liquid Plumber "Foaming Pipe Snake" down the slow bathtub drain, the phone rang.

"Is my mother there?" the voice said. It sounded too old to be one of their children.

"May I ask who's calling?"

"Her son?"

"And what is your name?"

"Chet."

"I'm sorry but that name doesn't ring a bell."

"My mother's name is Samantha. She lives with you. You married her, but before you were there, *I was here.*" The caller sounded like a fifteen-year-old who had spent much of his life alone, as, of course, he himself had. His heart went out to the deranged male teenager.

"I don't doubt it," he said.

"Don't try to mess with me," Chet said.

"I never try anything," he responded, surprising himself. "I don't know how to try things. I don't even wash my hands anymore.

I just hold them over the dry sink and think about cleaning them. Isn't that strange?"

He certainly felt strange speaking in this way to his, what—his stepson? Maybe there was no relation at all, since there could have been no intent behind the establishment of it. It had been so long since he had worked in an office, where he had learned so much about other people; if he hadn't turned to trading stocks on his computer to make his living, there's no telling how much better he would have handled this conversation.

Who wouldn't love a man like that? A man who had given up trying to wash his hands but who traded stocks on the Internet in an effective way? Yet he sometimes felt like something reproduced asexually, perhaps directly out of some stranger's testicle, just dangled to the ground by a groin shockwave.

"You're messing with me!" Chet said in a pathetic, imploring voice, as if this had been a long-standing problem between them.

He knew he had been misunderstood in some fundamental way; this was more or less always the case. But he had not meant to hurt the male teenager. Finally, he saw a way out: "I'm very sorry, Chet, but I will certainly tell her you called."

III.

One day he overheard his wife talking to someone on the phone in the kitchen.

"People dream about my cheesecake," she said into the phone.

He grabbed the spool of string from the kitchen drawer crammed with such things. There was something he needed to tie up, somewhere in the house.

"You're not listening to me," his wife said into the phone. "No you're not. . . I said I'm talking! I won't talk until I know you're listening. Are you listening?. . . Are you?"

Why had he married her? She could be crazy sometimes!

He occasionally called his old therapist and left messages on her voice mail. "It's happened," he would say, the cordless phone dropped into a dark sock to disguise his voice. "I've become who I thought I might be when I set out all those years ago."

He did this repeatedly until she called him back one day and left her own message in her inimitable high-pitched voice. "Stop it," she said.

It was a peculiarity of his personality that whatever he was called out about he stopped doing almost instantly. It was one of the reasons he didn't always regret having little contact with other people—because as soon as someone noted what he was doing, he was nearly incapable of doing it. This did not apply to trading securities because the stock market was all electronic, and the other computers that recorded his trades did not have what he would have called consciousness, so even though these computers held records of what he did, they did not really "see" it. He savored this. He followed twenty or so stocks on his computer, and what he learned through his computer told him what to do with them. He bought, sold, or held, depending, and by the end of the year he had a lot more money somehow. Trading stocks was the most stable and positive fact of his life.

In the first flush of his success as a stock trader, he had purchased from an antique dealer an ice ax used by Sir Edmund Hillary to climb Mount Everest in 1953. It cost three thousand dollars and came in a handsome mahogany box with a glass panel, so the ax could be seen. He thought of it as a tool that he used psychologically, in his stock trading and in his daily life, just by looking at it or thinking about it.

Once while he and his wife were watching a digital video his wife had taken of their son Edward's fifth birthday party, he (not his son) appeared in the left edge of the frame, viewed from behind. At first, he didn't recognize himself, but then his wife said, "Look at you."

"What?"

"Look at you," his wife repeated.

Why was she saying that? Was it the way his long neck held up his head like a waiter's wrist beneath a platter?

"What?" he asked again. But she never explained.

During the meat of the day, his real children were either in school or cared for by others. His wife had made the arrangements, though he was required to drive one way.

IV.

He continued making money with his computer for another three years, until it became obvious that his wife was having an affair. She had apologized for not telling him she had a separate son, but then she had taken up with a chef, of all people. This man cooked fish in a bag, she said, and who made bread just so, she said, and had a touch in bed that would curdle milk into cheese upon contact—she held back nothing when she wanted to hurt him.

"Oh, really?" he asked helplessly.

"Yes, really."

By this time, the tops of the drapes were caked with dust. No one had ever reached up there with the vacuum attachment, and no one had ever made the effort to remove the drapes and throw them into the wash machine. The implication was: he was home all day, why didn't he do it? He did many other things around the house, including dinner and laundry and small repairs, but he did not do that.

"And is that good or bad?" he said. "That sort of curdling touch, I mean?"

No answer. Which made him have to start over, stammering: "And when I saw you through that window, selling window coverings, are you saying that *that* wasn't really you, after all?"

"That reminds me," she said. "You never told me who you thought I was! When we met. Have you ever thought about that? Have you?"

"Yes, I have," he said, though he didn't remember her asking who he thought she was. "But I'm not going to tell you what I thought!" His voice had risen. He felt horrible. After all these years, his resolve to never stoop to her level had been broken.

"Well, then, the joke's on you, mister," she said. "It was never me. Don't you see? It was never me at all! You've been in love with yourself this whole time. Every window you've ever looked through, you've only seen yourself!"

"That's never been true!" he said. In fact, he hated himself. He wished their entire relationship had been filmed as evidence. "Many of the things you've said have been wrong!" he added, feeling savage and cruel, and it was, at long last, like dropping an atomic bomb from an airplane.

"There are things I want you to see about yourself," she responded calmly. "And I'm not a bit sorry."

He was so angry, his mind tripped over itself trying to formulate a response. He should have never let her go into his house ahead of him, no matter how exciting it had seemed; it was like being invaded by a fun-house mirror. He wanted to smash the mirror with his ax, but now that it had gotten inside of him, how could he do so without hurting himself?

Wild with anger, he stared into her eyes, but he stopped himself from saying more.

"Look at you," she said.

He gave himself over to thinking horrible things about her. He had never stooped so low. He struck at her in himself, again and again.

And still no one died! And still his hands hovered over the bone-dry sink!

The Bad Reader

Two grown men at the Dairy Queen consider a difficult case: a nephew gone astray, a gun brandished in a bookstore, shots fired. Red, the taller and older of the two men, wearing shorts and a blue polo shirt, stands by the plate-glass window, holding the stub end of his ice-cream cone at his side, in a nonlicking position. His hiked-up white athletic socks cover his bowlegged calves without a wrinkle; his posture is not unlike that of a transmission tower supporting high-tension wires. His companion, Bill, owner emeritus of Lapham Heating and Cooling, leans toward Red, holding his cone like a candle.

"Let's remember," Red says, "that my nephew himself admitted he can't see the world, that it doesn't come through to him, that all the malarkey he heard over at the university about the world being all language struck him as the most fanciful malarkey he'd ever heard, because the sad truth was that the world did not declare itself to him in words—that it just *was,* and he didn't know how to read it."

"So he can't see the world," Bill says, and he licks his ice cream.

"So he comes up to me at last year's Fourth of July picnic and says that despite the fact he can't actually see the world, can't say a recognizable word about it, he wants to become a 'fiction writer.'"

"And you said."

"I said don't give up what you've got going at the Sir Rents-A-Lot, no way. Stick it out there and you'll be fine. Write if you have to, just don't hurt any thing or any body."

"But he kept coming at you?"

"He kept coming at me because he considers me some kind of success in the world, and for some reason he never got into any of this with his old man, God rest his irritable soul. In fact, the boy's told me more than once that his old man could not see the world either and was only in it with difficulty. And me being his mother's only brother, well, he—"

"And you being a former high school football coach."

"Plus instructor of moral ethics and phys ed, don't forget, and pretty familiar with confused young men, I can tell you. In fact, I made my own perilous journey of personal discovery when I was his age—how I found my coaching vocation!"

"And there was no talking him back to our sense of reality? What we mean by it?"

On the other side of the counter, the Blizzard machine spins to life. It reminds Red of the whirring lawn mower blades that claimed this same nephew's right foot on his sixteenth birthday, and of his nephew's sour face when he refused the Xeroxes Red had made of appropriate rehab exercises.

"No talking him back whatsoever," Red says when the Blizzard machine stops. "So he starts burning the midnight oil after his days at Sir Rents-A-Lot, stays up all night reading Dostoevsky, and George Eliot, and Henry No-Time-for-Outdoor-Sports James. I tried to tell him, for one thing, that those folks have been pretty much forgotten by the undersixty set who's likely out there buying books. And for another, I said, get off the highbrow kick—like I told him going for that master's was adding insult to injury—and start on some of the more relaxed genres such as the mystery or the romance or the fantasy. You don't just reach for the top rung of the ladder and expect to end up on the roof already."

Bill, a hipless man, almost depantsed by the overstuffed wallet in his back pocket, hitches up his sagging khaki shorts with one hand. "And what'd he say?"

"He said that was a cruel way to talk to someone who couldn't see the world, like I was putting more feed in the trough of his despair. You know the funny thing, though? He took my advice about the fantasy story. Tried a short novel about a clan of talking cats trying to dam a river. Said it was a cross between *The Bridge over the River Kwai* and *Moby-Dick*."

"But with cats."

"That's right. It read like the fever dream of a ten-year-old girl. Sent it to a literary agent and got an incredibly polite but firm rejection letter, which he showed me."

"And it crushed him?"

"It did. He saw it as his last chance to talk in a public way about the world he couldn't read, and when he lost that—well, all he had was Sir Rents-A-Lot."

"Doesn't seem like much of a life."

"No, sir."

Red's ice cream has begun to drip, so he raises it for a few careful licks. He reflects briefly on how the path to self-actualization is not always clearly marked and many can't find their way.

"So when did you hear about the shooting?" Bill asks.

"Saw it on channel twelve. He wasn't my first thought, honestly.

My first thought was: we are a prosperous and insane nation, a prosperous and *therefore* insane nation—that's all I thought."

"Careful, Red," Bill says, raising a forefinger. "You must know that without small businessmen, we'd all be living in tepees and caves. What you really thought was, hey, it was a bookstore!"

"Yes, also, hey, it was a *bookstore*," Red says, laughing. "Who in this prosperous and insane nation of Donald Trumps and Timothy McVeighs and Martha Stewarts had ever heard of someone going postal in a bookstore? But there he is, blasting away in the fiction aisles. Shot every book with its cover turned out—"

"To promote greater sales," Bill adds knowingly.

"Don't think we're not on to how his mind works. I see his crazed and perpendicular logic all too clearly."

"Perpendicular?"

"Point was and is: he was killing books."

"A book killer. As if they were living things." Bill shakes his head.

"And apparently what he does is," Red rolls on, "while the book-buying public is facedown on the carpet, he goes out through the stockroom and onto a loading dock, where he ditches the gun, a wig, a sweater with Santa Claus and four of his reindeer on it, and a phony nose/glasses/mustache combo to be found an hour later—slyly slipped them into a trash can between the liner and the can itself! Nonchalantly enters the back forty of the parking lot like a man used to making no wake wherever he goes. No one's in pursuit—your bookstore people generally not the Rambo type—so I bet he just gets in his vehicle and leaves via the 'Celebration! Cinema' access road and then onto Milham, while the entire Portage police department arrives via Mall Drive, and so he disappears—and the shooting is on the news with the perp at large."

"But you're sure it's him."

"Eyewitnesses described the funny kind of walk we know to be a result of his plastic foot."

"Working at the Sir Rents-A-Lot as if nothing's happened."

"Hiding in plain view."

"I know he's your nephew, Red, but this young man is a danger to himself and others."

"That's my own point, Bill. Nephew-wise, this is as bad as it gets."

"We'd better get our butts over there."

Red and Bill finish their ice cream cones, request and knock back two Dixie cups of water, strap themselves into Bill's white Lincoln Town Car, and proceed from the Dairy Queen on West Michigan to the Sir Rents-A-Lot on West Main. The strip mall store sign displays a knight in armor on horseback, his battle lance skewering items for rent—TV, sofa, fridge. Out front, on the covered concrete walkway, sit couches and love seats with tears in their piping, or a chunk of skirt missing, or some recalcitrant stain.

Despite Red's hope of presenting a cool, streetwise front to the shooter, the bells ring as the door opens and he and Bill have to weave and jerk down a crooked path through the jumbled merchandise toward the counter in back. The showroom has most types of furniture and appliances except bookcases. TVs are the prevalent item, some with flat screens five feet wide, all tuned to the same rap video with the sound muted. The dressers and coffee tables tend to be detailed with gold and silver: there are two mirrors shaped like ocean waves, and one gray dresser top Red passes has a laminate coating like what you'd find on a nonstick fry pan, with a scratch shaped like a hockey stick.

Red's nephew, Albert, stands in the back. As they approach him, he gathers up several sheets of paper and stuffs them under the counter. He's got the wiry body and skull-like head of a deranged

QUALITY SNACKS / 166

marathoner—the only sort of athlete Red cannot abide. But Red knows the young man has no regimen whatsoever; he suspects, in fact, that Albert has *thought* himself into this physical shape. The young man's short black hair has thinned since the last time Red saw him, and he's wearing a blue Sir Rents-A-Lot polo shirt and tan chinos, absently cupping his hands together as if packing a snowball.

"What are you willing to explain and what are you afraid to admit?" Red asks heatedly. "Because I don't think you have a good excuse for what you've done against the public."

"Hi, Uncle Red," Albert says. He nods a generic greeting toward Bill, who returns the nod with a slightly bug-eyed look on his face.

"You take the fact of your self-invented failings too hard," Red says. "It's self-pitying to say you can't see the world—when you definitely can."

Albert sighs. "I can sort of see it, but not in a meaningful way."

"Go ahead, *persist*," Bill says. "We're not here to talk you out of it. We're just here to see your type of animal in action." He folds his arms.

"Bill's good people, Albert," Red says, low and confidential. "Friend of mine from the DQ."

"A friend who happens to have a few questions," Bill adds.

"Such as," Red says, "where were you on the afternoon of June the fourteenth? That would be yesterday."

"I was at home. Writing."

"About feral cats with a bent for civil engineering?" Red asks.

"Something else, actually."

"Something else. Can you prove that?"

"Of course not," Albert says.

"What's on those papers you put under the counter?"

Red hears the cruel battering edge in his voice but can't help himself. It's the way into the center of every young man he has ever known, into their veritable stinking bedrooms, where he finds dreams in the posters on the walls and the means to achieve them gathering dust in the closet. How often has Red turned the bracing fire hose of his truth on such hapless malcontents? "What?" he demands. "A sworn statement for the police?"

"I'd be happy to read it to you," Albert says. Apparently the prospect makes him smile.

"Never allow a man to set the terms of his own interrogation," Red says dogmatically. He glances at Bill to see how this bit of ad hoc wisdom has come across, but Bill's eyes are locked onto Albert like a pair of tractor beams. Red almost says, *Get your own crazy nephew!*

"Well, well, well," Bill says. "I'd like to hear this fictional story."

"It's not exactly a story," Albert says.

"Then what is it?" Red asks.

Albert pulls the papers out from under the counter. "Let me just read it."

Red and Bill exchange glances, Red trying to see in Bill's eyes whether they're being outfoxed. Red breaks first: "Fine, let's hear it. Let's hear what you wrote down while your doppelgänger was on a shooting spree at the bookstore."

Albert purses his lips and narrows his eyes at Red.

"All right now, easy, son," Bill says.

"'The Bad Reader,'" reads Albert. "'By Albert Taft.'" He clears his throat. "'I love seeing how the world seems with you. When you describe someone's belt buckle or the flat of someone's forearm or the way someone's hand curls in her lap like the way hands curl in laps in paintings of the Italian sixteenth century, that's when I love you and want to be like you and be in your world. Or when one of your characters is standing in her black tights at the bus stop, heading uptown, or making some penetrating remark about men, or describing the contents of her purse—receipts, Peruvian keepsake, cosmetics, and prescription pills, the details of which reveal more about the human soul than all the psychology books ever written. Or when she's talking to some man who is pretty cool but always somewhat dumber than her in all the important emotional ways, but has charm, sort of. Or when I know she's ridden horses. That's when I want to love you very much and be in your world with you.'"

"I thought you said this was a story," Bill interjects.

Albert stiff-arms Bill with a quick glance and continues: "'I cannot describe my own world at all. In fact, when I try, I say things like: "It was dots and black." Or, "The surge fucked me over." Or, "my apartment." I say, "my apartment"—and freeze. The sunlight is always different, but I cannot describe the differences. The sky above this dismal Midwestern city is always different, but I cannot tell how. I know my favorite abstractions: implosion, down. I know my favorite smells, but I cannot describe them. But when I read the way you have written: *Under the dog's collar was the smell of an athletic sock that has spent three years beneath the crawl space of a porch,* that's when I love you and want to be in your world—however much I know this is wrong.'"

"Is this about a girl?" Red interrupts. He wants no part of the boy's cockamamie writing. Best to punch through to the essence of the case. "Are all these problems just because you're not getting laid?"

Albert rolls his eyes. "This piece is in the voice of a character," he says. "This character is not necessarily me. It's just someone talking."

"I'm just saying relationships are a problem we can talk sense about, if you want to." Red shrugs theatrically.

Albert ignores him and reads on: "'The problem is that I don't seem to exist, yet you seem to exist very vividly, and everything you touch is charged with something. I dream of you noticing me, but in fact *I have to read you* to be in any vivid world at all. You're so un-self-consciously current and "with it," and other readers immediately note that the world you represent is the world as it is, right now. In fact, I don't see the world at all until you say it, but when you do say it, I want to be in it. Many times I have been fooled by this feeling of wanting to be in your world, because it seems very much like love, and I know what's very possible to think about me: he's simply a frustrated worm in love—'"

"Ah, there it is," Red says. "I predicted it!"

"'The exact problem, though, is that I am not in love with you. Or the problem is that, if I am, it is beside the point. It *has* to be beside the point. Because we've never met. Because I only know about you through your words, which are separate from you yourself. Who are unknowable. Which makes me mad.'"

"Sounds like a lot of jealousy and resentment to me," Bill mutters.

Red opens a hand chest-high to invite Bill to pipe down.

"'I guess what I am saying is that I would like to be you, but I am always me. I would like to have my own world, but I don't know how to see or say it. In more ways than one, *I can't tell what's happening.* This is the fastest way to become enraged that I know of, and some day I will explode.'"

"Did he just say 'explode'?" Bill whispers.

"Shh!" Red hisses. "He's digging his own grave just fine!"

Red would like this grave dug completely, to be sure—the boy must be broken down before Red can build him back up—but he has no interest in standing face-to-face with Albert at the bottom of such a hole. Yet the carpeted floor feels as if it's sliding away under his feet. The sensation reminds him of learning to surf off the Baja peninsula, battling the dangerous waves and currents of his own restless youth—before his coaching vocation took hold.

"'If you ever read this,'" Albert continues, "'don't hold it against me that I have to explode. In this way—and only in this way, I'm afraid—I can become interesting, but only through your description of my explosion, and not through the fact of my explosion itself. Please describe all you can about me. I want to be vivid, but in fact I am abstract.'"

Albert recedes into silence, surprisingly close to tears.

"Listen, Mr. Abstraction," Red says, grateful for the practiced belittling tone that covers the unease he feels. "There are dating services for young men your age. But first you've got to get over this *anger*."

"These things right here," Bill says excitedly. "What you work with day in and day out—these couches, love seats, wash machines and TVs; these DVD players and fridges and microwaves. *These* are the things of the world. Just look at them. Can't you *see* them?"

"When you name them, that's fine," Albert says with the sort of cheap world weariness that has always made Red want to knock in someone's teeth. "It's obvious that they're there, but they make no sense to me."

"Let's go," Bill says with disgust. "He can't be helped."

"You're just being stubborn," Red says to Albert. "And what kind of lunatic story was that? Who's the bad reader? Who's this woman you're talking to? I wouldn't be surprised if she's a nice regular gal who just happened to give your morose ass the boot! This is willfully courting insanity. I won't have it! I'm your uncle and I don't accept where things stand right now!"

"No one's asking you to accept anything," Albert says evenly.

"And what if there'd been a security guard with his wits about him?" Red barrels on. "You'd be dead right now—and for shooting up a bookstore, no less, attacking one of the great institutions of our—"

"Uncle Red," Albert says more loudly, hand upraised. His glance pierces Red. "You'll have to excuse me. I've got some inventory to do." He picks up a clipboard and walks out from behind the counter and into the merchandise. The hitch in his gait makes it seem as if one foot has stepped into something softer than the other.

Bill eyes the door and begins to shuffle as if he's got ants in his pants. Red feels a twinge of doubt. He and Bill were on the brink of knocking the scales from the boy's eyes, inducing the youngster to take some sort of pledge to become a different person, but what if Albert would act to keep those scales in place?

"No one need know about this visit," Red says in a low voice to Bill. "It may not be for us to arrest, legislate against, or even necessarily discourage the rogue elements of our society." Then he raises his voice a bit: "We can only hope that our encounter with young Albert here has planted a seed of some kind that will one day—"

"What was that?" Albert says, turning abruptly toward Red.

"Just speaking my mind," Red throws back. "Last time I checked, there was freedom of speech and assembly."

"Not in a private place of business," Albert says. "You here to rent something?"

"Not likely!" Red laughs. "What's your effective interest rate? A hundred percent a year, give or take?"

"Then I'll have to ask you to leave."

"Are you going to call the fuzz?" Bill asks, stepping forward.

"There *are* laws against loitering," Albert says.

"Well," Red says, "some so-called lawful actions are morally *unconscionable*, such as disrespecting your uncle."

Albert pretends he hasn't heard, scribbling something on his clipboard. Then he clicks his pen closed and strides back toward the counter.

"I'll tell you what's unconscionable," Albert says. He reaches down to a shelf under the register and brings up a small handgun, which he places on the counter.

The gun attracts all eyes. Albert allows a thin, creepy smile to spread across his face.

"Listen," Bill says, "life is inherently precious."

"Not when you can't tell what it is," Albert replies.

"He's making a play for sympathy," Red whispers to Bill.

Albert wheels on Red and shouts, "Put a sock in it, old man!"

Red feels as though he's been struck with an electric cattle prod. His lips tremble. His face begins to sweat. He manages to speak, looking at no one in particular: "How long will you act with such violence and rage and disrespect, hotshot? That's no way to be in the world!"

"Who says?" Albert asks.

"I say!" Bill bursts out. "We all say. The reason you can't see the world and have all these women troubles is you don't love your own gosh-darned self."

"Who said I've got women troubles?" Albert shouts. "Who says I don't love me?" He coughs. "I love myself fine. If it were just me, I'd be completely happy—get rid of all the assholes and I wouldn't have a care in the world."

"Then why write such depressing crapola?" says Red. "Why shoot up a bookstore? Why try to—"

"Don't antagonize me," Albert says. He picks up the gun and aims two-handed at a twenty-seven-inch Samsung. His closed mouth twists to the left. There is a loud crack and a tinkling of glass.

"Jesus Christ!" Red yells, his ears ringing. "Put that damn thing down! Don't you understand the true way to be? Don't you understand morality?"

"Damn it, Red," Bill says. "No one cares about morality anymore."

"I care," Albert and Red say simultaneously, and then they make eye contact.

Albert suddenly ducks behind the counter, out of sight.

"Oh, for god's sake!" Bill says. "Let's get out of here."

Red says nothing. He tries to be still and listen his way behind the counter, where there is no apparent movement. He'd been on the brink of reestablishing his grip on the boy and now this.

"Dabgummit, Albert!" Red says. "What are you hiding from?"

The ensuing silence is like a dirty shoe to Red's face. He's always hated disengagement during coachable moments.

"Are you some kind of *coward*?" Red adds. "I bet you're scared!"

Charging a young man with fear is certainly a time-honored coaching tactic, and Red hopes this will cut through the lad's resistance, bring him to his senses, set him on the long road to full socialization and rudimentary happiness. He looks to Bill for confirmation, but Bill is staring at the counter, his lips pulled back in a fairly hideous grimace.

"You're right," Albert finally says, still hidden. "I am a coward. I don't like how I see, but I don't know how to be different, and I don't have the guts to live with that."

"Well, that's a start," Red says with some relief. "We can talk sense about—"

A gunshot explodes from behind the counter.

"Goddamn it!" Bill says. "Jesus, Mary, and Joseph!"

"Albert?" Red shouts.

Both he and Bill can't seem to move.

"Albert!"

"Let's get clear of this," Bill says. "Nothing you ever want to look at. Come on—let's go!"

"We can't leave him," Red says. "He's my nephew."

"And he almost shot us, and no one will be the wiser if we take off right now. Do you have any idea the paperwork involved in find-ing a dead body? They'll want to know what we said and did here."

"We could've saved him," Red says.

"Aw, wake up, you ninny! Nobody ever saved anybody!"

But Red doesn't even give Bill a menacing glare. Instead, he takes a step toward the counter. He's sure Albert's remains will be back there: inert, unforgettable, a certain failure now. The boy had wanted that woman to describe his explosion, but of course she's also nowhere to be seen—if she ever existed.

Red pauses and listens. He imagines he hears water purling over rocks in a slow-moving stream, as if he's out somewhere in nature, exploring. Someone ought to see what's behind the counter pretty soon, he thinks. A coach is simply the most responsible adult in any situation. He takes another step. But he realizes that stepping is one thing and looking is another and what comes after looking is even worse.

Always the Same Dream

In the dream, I'm always eating a bacon, lettuce, and tomato sand-wich on the green-line L train when a woman carrying a boa con-strictor gets on at thirty-fifth Street. She sits across from me wearing a bobcat-print pair of stretch pants and a tiger-print top. She has her hair pulled up in an alarmingly vertical ponytail, kind of like Pebbles Flintstone, and get this, after she puts away her smartphone and lets the snake wrap itself around a pole, she busts out a bacon, lettuce and tomato sandwich—just like mine.

I always wake up inside my body, on the bed, in the indentation I've made in my side of the mattress. My wife and I lie next to each other like Iowa and Nebraska. It takes me hours of driving across myself to reach her, sometimes.

There is a cyst in my brain in the left front-temporal region. It appears to be growing. My neurologist is keeping an eye on it. He's been talking of draining it via needle aspiration or burr hole. If necessary.

The doorbell rings and I'm down the stairs in my blue jeans

and a T-shirt that I've laundered to translucency. I have a job as a metallurgist, but I am home today, taking a breather.

At the door is a tall, brown-haired woman with a zig-zagging part down the center of her head. She's wearing a powder-blue, short-sleeve shirt with navy khakis and a mannish belt. Her tan arms go nicely with the powder-blue. She's beautiful in a straight-haired, smiley-eyed sort of way.

"I'm here to read the gas meter," she says. Her name patch reads, "Sherrey."

"Never seen it spelled that way," I say.

"Your meter?" she says pointedly.

"It's down in the basement," I say. "It squeaks when it lets the gas in." I lead her to the basement door, flick the light switch, and let her go down first. "Watch your head," I say.

In my dream, I am always about to get head from my wife, but something intervenes: all the cupcakes must get frosted, the plane must come to a complete stop at the gate, the jar of tea must steep in the sun.

The previous owners walled off a darkroom down here, using up most of the floor space. She squeezes sideways between the laundry table and the staircase to get to the meter.

"It squeaks when our gas comes in. I don't know if that's a problem or not. It probably isn't—"

My work as a metallurgist often involves determining whether certain coatings on certain metals will fail under certain conditions. It's possible that the mind-set I cultivate to do this work has contributed to a hyper-conscientiousness, in all things.

"It's the dials on your meter that squeak," she says.

She reads the meter and punches the numbers into a handheld electronic device.

"Thank you for helping me make sense of things," I say.

.   .   .

When things start to go wrong, there are signs: shouting in the car—check; wishing death for your enemies and massive windfalls for yourself—check; holding yourself hostage until the Stockholm Syndrome kicks in—check.

Who would have thought that metallurgical work would pale, after a time? Who would have thought that my efforts to promote positive interpersonal relationships among my colleagues would backfire? Now the break room has become hell and my coworkers have taken to calling me "The Poet," although I do not read or write poetry. This all started when I asked certain individuals not to bully me or others at our place of work. I have become a sort of interpersonal whistle-blower, on the premises. I fear my expertise in the areas of ferrous metallurgy, heat treating, coatings, nondestructive testing, and failure analysis may not be enough to preserve my job.

.   .   .

Every night it's the same dream: I am juggling fire sticks in my living room when the ceiling catches ablaze. I realize my wife is on the second floor. I yell up the stairs, "Honey, the house is on fire! Time to ramble!" No answer. I leave and walk four blocks to the nearest Walgreens, get a bag of Nacho Doritos, and sit on a concrete wheel stop out front. I call my wife's cell phone. No answer. Overcome with guilt, I don't even finish the Doritos. Always the same dream.

.   .   .

Every night it's the same dream: I'm playing in a charity softball game, batting against Abraham Lincoln and Mother Teresa. He's a rightie and she's a leftie, so they pitch together, side by side, each with a hand on the ball. Lincoln and Mother Teresa leave a floater over the plate, and I hit a line drive that caroms off the side of Mother Teresa's head, knocking her down. Lincoln dashes his top hat to the turf in disgust. No one fields the ball, but I'm frozen, unable to run to first or to go to Mother Teresa's assistance. The ball remains in play. Every night the same dream!

. . .

My wife thinks it's significant that my brain cyst began growing at about the same time I became an interpersonal whistle-blower at work. Often when I explain why I feel compelled to confront certain people about certain things, she makes points that echo why my coworkers find me to be a pain in the ass. I have tried to mediate petty feuds regarding design credits, line downtime, botched batches; I have inadvertently insulted men who have made insensitive speeches; I have implied that I have noticed hypocrisies among women and men. I have occasionally defended myself against disrespect and hostility. It would be nice to be told that I have behaved well, that I am not, in fact, the problem.

"Mind your own business," my wife says.

"Some of it is directly my business. Some indirectly."

"Let it go," my wife says.

"I've let many things go," I say. I do not tell her that, for example, I let go the time a coworker called me a "dick" when, after an inspection, I detailed to him the potential consequences of the non-spec tolerances on a new touch-control electronic transmission shifter production line under his supervision. She would say that I *shouldn't* have let *that* go. My "let go versus confront" decision-making process is apparently broken, with disastrous inter- and intrapersonal consequences.

. . .

There is a fissure in my relationship with my wife through which, I suspect, other women are trying to emerge.

.   .   .

During waking hours, I'm down at the hardware store, among the nuts and bolts, trying to finger my way into something small and secure. A woman wearing a T-shirt with a map of Oregon on the back accidentally elbows me and then, impulsively it seems, tickles my ribs. Without wasting time, I take her to lunch at Applebee's. She orders the surf-and-turf combo with fried mozzarella sticks as an appetizer. I order a chicken Caesar salad, and when the food comes, I go to the rest room, where I become emotionally ill. I stand in front of the mirror, lifting my hair off my forehead, looking for signs of my cyst, though I know it is trapped by my skull.

.   .   .

Then I'm at the neurologist's office and I'm telling him that this brain cyst is literally eating my mind, and the doctor says, "Inappropriate laughter is one of the seven signs of dementia."

I say, "Oh yeah, what are the other six?"

And that's when he says, "For this test, you must be completely unconscious."

He gases me and I black out.

.   .   .

I know I'm going to pull out of this horrible depression because every night it's the same dream: I'm spinning sugar into cotton candy when the doorbell rings. It's a woman dressed as a trout and then it becomes clear she *is* a trout, only she has the face of Gwen Stefani. Her gills are throbbing weakly. Her biggest fin splays against the door. "I'm suffocating," she says.

"My god, would you like some cotton candy!" I scream.

She doesn't answer.

Every night.

.　　.　　.

At work, I have one remaining friend, a fellow alum from the Illinois Institute of Technology, who sees all of my shit in 3-D, well before I am aware of it.

"You've got bad mental habits," she told me the other day in the break room. She had just polished off a bag of microwave popcorn and was wiping her fingers on some napkins. "You're going to kill yourself."

"I am not," I said.

"It won't be a conventional suicide," she said tendentiously. "You're going to kill yourself just by thinking the way you do. The body/mind partnership is tricky. When a person's thoughts get too destructive, the body tries to disconnect from the mind to protect itself, and ironically this can make you sick. When it gets really bad, the body can stop cooperating with the mind altogether. And this is super dangerous because critical functions like breathing are controlled by both the autonomic nervous system, which is how the body regulates itself, and the volitional nervous system, which is how the mind moves the body. The problem is, sometimes the body overshoots trying to escape the mind, and the autonomic baby gets thrown out with the volitional bath water. See? Worst case, you stop breathing in your sleep and die.

"So you've got to be careful with everything that goes on in your mind, Jerry. Seriously."

"Thank you for helping me make sense of things," I said.

.　　.　　.

Every night it's the same dream: in a hurry to buy a Mountain Dew at Walgreens, I run over a four-year-old boy playing with a tennis ball in the street. His body gets stuck somehow in the back-left wheel well. I try to pull him out but it's no-go, so I continue to Walgreens despite a horrible rubbing sound that seems to emanate from the trunk (but I know better). When I pull into the parking lot, there's a police officer waiting for me. "What's *that* all about?" he asks, pointing to the obstructed wheel well. Always the same dream!

.   .   .

My therapist tells me over and over: there's no point to all of this negativity. What good has it done you? Why can't you think more positively? And so I do. But then night falls.

.   .   .

I spend a nervous morning drawing with a ballpoint pen the flags of the five permanent members of the United Nations Security Council. Then my wife drives me to the neurologist's office. It's time to aspirate the cyst, to be on the safe side.

"Things can only get better," she says.

I no longer tell her what's happening at work because I cannot bear to have her side with my enemies. This has improved our day-to-day relationship, but at a cost.

"Sorry for all of the shouting," I say. "I haven't been myself."

"I know," she says. "That's just the cyst talking."

We pull into the parking garage of the hospital and switchback through several dimly lit levels, looking for a spot.

"God, I hope this does it!" I exclaim and burst into tears.

.   .   .

It now seems clear to me that bad dreams help us to develop a healthy relationship to guilt: when we wake up from a bad dream, the relief we feel is so profound that it is one of the higher pleasures of being alive. The experience of the bad thing is so vivid and the realization that it didn't actually happen is so pleasurable that you get positive and negative reinforcement in one intense package: you welcome the innocent feeling; you want to avoid the nightmare at any cost. It is always the same dream.

No Joy in Santa's Village

It was the bottom of the ninth and Santa was down 43–1. After playing every position, taking every at bat, all game, he was tired. He was six for thirty-one with one run batted in, himself, in the seventh, on a fading drive down the right-field line that had curved around the foul pole at 353 feet. He'd taken his base trot slower than anyone had ever taken it. He was tired and he was resting himself. He'd been glad to hit the home run, but he was also very tired.

By special order of the commissioner, he wore his red suit without a number, though by this last inning he'd taken off his coat to reveal a gray thermal undershirt and suspenders. Tonight he was battling the Cubs at Wrigley, yet he had last at bats: Santa didn't have his own stadium, so for half of his games he was designated "the home team."

His dugout was filled with elves. Some never moved, some never sat still—whittling a piece of wood into a bat, whittling the bat into baseballs, whittling the baseballs into tiny bats, which were whittled into still tinier baseballs. Some were incontinent, some respired entirely through their pores, like plants. Some rooted for Santa, some cast spells against him. At each game they created a locked-ward atmosphere in the dugout. Last year, one or another of the elves would occasionally streak onto the field in the middle of a game, tear up a piece of turf, and retreat toward the bench, gibbering hysterically, holding the turf aloft. Now wire mesh closed off Santa's dugout from the field. Sometimes the elves wouldn't let him back into his own dugout, hanging on from the inside to the handle of the screen door that only Santa could unlock. People wondered why he traveled with so many elves since they didn't play and were as likely to root for him as they were to heckle him. But the idea of playing the game completely alone was more than he could bear.

In the Transpolar Baseball League there is no slaughter rule, and Santa was lucky he had a wicked knuckleball or he would have given up thousands of runs a game. In fact, his ERA was 39.238, though he led the league in strikeouts, averaging 20 per game. Since he didn't have a catcher, he took an old toy sack filled with baseballs to the mound with him. Umpires hated Santa because they had to take every pitch he threw directly on their chest protectors. As a result, most umps padded themselves like hockey goalies when Santa was on the mound; they wore small, old-fashioned mitts to catch or deflect his pitches.

Even though he was by all accounts more than 150 years old, Santa was actually an excellent pitcher, but having to man the entire field by himself hobbled him defensively. In a nod to the childlike innocence Santa had brought back to the game, he was granted "pitcher's mitt out," just the way kids often played it in neighborhood pickup games all over the world. This meant that if Santa fielded the ball before the runner reached first base, the runner would be out. It also meant that as soon as Santa had chased down a hit, whether it was bobbling across the warning track in right field or sitting still in the soft grass in center, the runners would have to stop advancing. Santa had the thighs of a soccer player.

He also had two sane elf assistants, Ube Trindle and Dinker Underdale, who were allowed outside the dugout. Dinker was a large female elf who hoped someday to marry Santa, and Ube, a male, had dreamed of being a major leaguer. They roamed behind the umpire when Santa was on the mound, gathering up deflected pitches and collecting them in a toy bag to trade with Santa when he needed to replenish his baseball supply.

Santa, of course, could have simply played for one of the established teams. But, surprisingly, Santa was not a team player. And the fans—the entire Transpolar Baseball League—were fascinated and provoked by his hubris.

So Santa at the bat, down 43–1, with two out, nobody on, bottom of the ninth.

The Cubs' ace, Clint Overman, leaned in for the sign, a lupine grimace on his face. One out away from a complete game, he seemed to derive a sick pleasure from the prospect of sending Santa home at the end of another winless season. (In two years, Santa had yet to win a single game.) A line of spectators shook a banner in right field. Santa knew what it said—he'd seen the same banner in the same part of the park from Seattle to Tampa—but he couldn't help but glance over: "Santa = Genocide." "Santa" was spelled with red and green letters; "Genocide," of course, was in black.

The elves holding the banner remembered the times before Kris Kringle had entered their ancient settlement on the western coast of Greenland. They remembered how Kris, in the wake of his victory in the 1870 All-Elf Toy Building Competition, convinced the elves to let him give his prize-winning trompe l'oeil–painted 250-box car wooden train set to his nephew in Denmark, instead of destroying it, as had been the elf custom for centuries. For the elves, such destruction was a way of "emphasizing process over product" and fertilizing future creativity. But Santa had cunningly argued for the revolutionary proposition that "distribution is destruction," citing for authority the Latin roots of these words: *distribuere* [*dis-*, **apart** + *tribuere*, **to give**] and *destruere* [*de-*, **away** + *struere*, **to pile up**]. Because didn't *destroy*, "to pile up away," really mean "distribute" and conversely didn't *distribute*, "to give apart," really mean "destroy"? Both meant getting rid of the toys, and isn't that what the elves wanted?

Suddenly overwhelmed with memories of the day he left Greenland for good—warehouses burning near the docks at Paamiut Harbor, elves keening mournfully like seagulls—Santa raised his right hand and stepped out of the batter's box before Overman could go into his windup. The umpire declared a time-out, and boos rained down from the stands. There was supposed to be a tremendous fireworks display after the game, and the crowd was anxious for it.

Santa didn't know what he longed for anymore.

Apparently inspired by the boos, one girl yelled in a shrill voice, "You forgot the batteries!" Another boy, maybe her brother, screamed, "I didn't want any shirts!"

Santa squinted toward the box seats on the first-base side and immediately spotted the two naughty children. He pulled his lips into his mouth to keep himself from delivering a stinging rebuke. He knew he couldn't answer these ungracious criticisms without embarrassing the parents who had actually purchased those gifts. The truth was, Santa no longer made nor delivered presents. He had retired from gift giving and turned to baseball because no one believed he could deliver so many presents in one night, and so people had, more and more over the years, gotten used to making their own arrangements for gifts—trusting Amazon.com, and Radio Shack, and Sony, and Schwinn, and Hasbro, and Mattel and Eddie Bauer and Lands' End before they would trust the aging miracle man. But maybe more importantly, Santa's notion of the loss leader—giving a single free gift to inculcate the habit of Christmas gift giving between all members of the population—had worked all too well. His industrialist partners had grown fat and no longer needed him.

The genocide banner, of course, had never lost its power to rankle. Ironically, fielding a team composed of himself and a squad of elves was supposed to help make amends for what he'd done to the elves and their culture. Santa's desire for personal redemption, in turn, had dovetailed with the league's interest in the wholesome image Santa would bring to a game damaged by interminable doping scandals. But league officials had grown wary when they realized that the tiny elves offered virtually no strike zone. Nervous owners foresaw endless innings of elves drawing walk after walk, the fans insane with tedium. In the end, the commissioner ruled that the elves failed the height requirement and proposed instead that Santa handpick the balance of his lineup from the legions of mall Santas from all across the country, as fielding a true professional expansion club was beyond his resources.

Though Santa had known some of these men for years, barking orders at them over shortwave radio, telling them to telegram him some list or another ASAP, he couldn't bring himself to take the field with them. Surrogate Santa informants were a necessary evil in a global distribution network. But now his "territory" comprised thirty ballparks, all in a relatively condensed swath of North America, only one of which would he need to visit on any given day, over a season that spanned half a year instead of one night. With detailed maps of the world still underpinning every waking thought, the playing fields themselves seemed embarrassingly small. Where was the challenge in manning a single position? The slow pace of the game would be an insult to his amazingly proficient central nervous system, which allowed flawless high-speed multitasking to a degree only otherwise possible with today's advanced computers. (Dutch neurologists had determined that Santa harnessed up to 73 percent of his brain.) Only playing every position by himself would make such a pace respectable. Santa would go it alone.

Now as the disenchanted elves in right field intensified their taunts and accusations, a hardcore band known as "Santa's Helpers," who followed Santa across the country in huge ancient Chrysler New Yorkers or mural-embossed Chevy vans and VW buses, panhandling the price of tickets—these good people rose in the left-field bleachers and hoisted a sixty-foot banner of their own, which read, "We Believe in Santa Claus!"

Santa stepped back into the batter's box, set one foot, then the other.

The windup, and the pitch.

It was a curveball, low and outside, and Santa let it ride. He rested the bat on his right shoulder and rocked back on his heels, bouncing on his knees a little bit.

The next pitch was a fastball, up and in. It brushed Santa off the plate. He shouted a few choice words at Overman, pulled on his beard to show his anger, and took a step as if he would rush the mound. No one was fooled. Being Santa, he would never rush the mound. Still, wouldn't it be nice to see Santa rush the mound, just once?

Fastball. Fouled off behind the plate.

"Get it over with, Santa!" a woman screamed from somewhere down the third-base line. "For God's sake, end this!"

"Pack it in, Santa. Pack it in!" This from a ten-year-old boy between cupped hands.

Everyone knew this might be his last game. There had been rumors. Three hundred and twenty-three consecutive losses would take a toll on any man. Why not quit? Or he could give in and sign a contract with some other team. He could start in any rotation in the league. If he chose the right club, he might play in a World Series some day. He might have a catcher leap into his arms.

Santa fouled off another pitch. The count was two and two. He could just stand there with his bat on his shoulder and the next pitch could end the season, his entire career. He wondered: "Do I have a self-destructive streak?"

He called another time-out and stepped out of the box, as if to give himself a chance to contemplate all questions. He leaned his bat against his groin and refastened the Velcro of his white batting glove. He picked up the bat and twisted his powerful hands around on the grip. The bat did not feel totally right. He looked toward his dugout. Dinker Underdale crouched on one knee near the on-deck circle. Santa tapped the bat barrel twice with one finger, and Dinker sprinted over with a new piece of lumber.

Santa beamed at her as they exchanged bats. Dinker blushed and said, "You are the most productive human in the world." Then she darted back, retaking her spot next to Ube Trindle, whose eyes were aflame with naked, multileveled envy.

Santa felt fortified. "Come on, suck it up," he told himself, digging in his front foot. "Get back in the game." He raised his bat and waggled it with an expectant looseness that might tighten into power at any instant.

The windup, and the pitch.

Santa hit a line drive back up the middle. Overman's glove speared the air, but the ball skipped into center field. A few elves slammed into the mesh, keening loudly. Santa rounded first and retreated to the bag. He called the expected time-out and trotted back to home plate.

Santa's baserunning was performed by the Santa Simulation

System. Instead of granting Santa a pinch runner, the umpires would run a computer simulation of what the Santa-on-base would do if, say, the next pitch to Santa were low and outside (would he have taken a decent lead, would he make a break for second?) or if Santa hit a sharp grounder deep into the shortstop's hole. The simulations were based on measurements taken of Santa before the game and updated during the seventh-inning stretch: How fast was Santa in the ninety-foot dash? How was his reaction time, his vertical leap? How would those skills deteriorate throughout the game based on how much activity Santa had performed? How could they be improved by momentum, crowd reaction, luck?

For the benefit of the defense and the fans, large screens were hung from the upper deck and above the lawn in the dead-center-field bleachers, with smaller stand-up versions behind first and third base, screens which showed what the imaginary Santas were doing during the play. These screens were supplemented with ear-pieces worn by the defense, which gave relevant fielders shorthand verbal descriptions (in English, Spanish, or Japanese) of the where-abouts of imaginary Santas. The left fielder would hear, for instance, if an imaginary Santa were trying to make it from first to third on a single to the gap. The ball itself carried a wireless transmitter that provided most of the variables that drove the simulations. The main difficulty was establishing a definitive relation between the imaginary Santas, which existed only on screens, and the actual ball on the actual playing field. The imaginary Santa might try a hook slide. The third baseman would listen to know where to place the tag. How to tell for sure that the real had touched the imaginary?

Santa retrieved his bat from foul territory and once again took up his stance in the batter's box. The imaginary Santa at first took a decent lead.

"Pack it in, Santa!" rang out sporadically from points around the stadium, like flashbulbs popping.

Santa's Helpers got a faint call and response going among two sections of the bleachers: "Do you believe?" "We believe!" "Do you believe?" "WE BELIEVE!!!"

There was nothing that focused Santa more than having imaginary Santas on base. That sense of being in many places at once was very catalyzing. Why not score a few runs right here? he thought. It ain't over till it's over.

Santa decided he would hit behind the runner. The imaginary Santa was going on the pitch. The real Santa got something he could work with over the outside part of the plate and promptly stroked a line drive down the right-field line, and the ball bounced all the way to the wall. The right fielder had been playing him to pull but got over in a hurry and fielded the ball cleanly. The imaginary Santa rounded third and headed for home. As Santa himself did a stand-up slide into second base, the cutoff man wheeled and threw to the plate. The imaginary Santa dove face-first. The catcher took the throw on one skip and swept the tag. Not in time. The crowd, almost involuntarily, was on its feet. More elves hit the mesh. Other elves turned their backs on the field and threw their hands forward in disgust.

This was exciting baseball. The bipartisan scoreboard bloomed: "santa SANTA **SANTA**!!!!"

I'm everywhere at once again, thought Santa with satisfaction, heading back to home plate. He pumped both fists alternately in the air and shook his tail feathers a bit. This was known as "The Santa Salute," and it always provoked the fans.

Santa once again dug in against Overman. "I have special powers," he murmured to the catcher, and they watched Overman's next offering dip a fraction below the knees. Santa had a good eye. Ball one.

"That's not what Mrs. Claus said," the catcher dryly remarked, and he tossed the ball back to the pitcher.

Santa fouled off the next pitch in such a way that the ball ricocheted off the catcher's mask. The catcher called a time-out. Santa had a moment to reflect on what he'd seen during that pitch: the ball approaching almost in slow motion, every stitch of the seams visible, as if he could have autographed the ball as it went by, but instead he used his precise knowledge of the ball's position to take revenge on the catcher.

The next pitch also arrived very slowly, seemingly adjusting its flight to meet with the fat part of his bat. He made sweet crushing contact, and the ball arced into the left-field bleachers, without a doubt. Joy among Santa's Helpers. He took the bases briskly. His heart pumped in huge spasms, each of which seemed to supply enough blood to last a week. He had the old familiar sensation that he was accelerating while time was slowing down. Whenever he got a rally going, he seemed to gain confidence, speed, and concentration. It was the feeling he'd had during those Christmas Eves all those years ago when his production/distribution network was reaching peak activity.

During his next five at-bats, he methodically sprayed singles and doubles all over the park. The score was now 43–8. The Cubs sent in a relief pitcher. The fans began to get more interested—in some cases, despite themselves. Who could resist rooting for Santa, deep down?

Though purists had denounced Santa as a gimmick, he had boosted attendance among office workers who had absorbed the tasks of "downsized" colleagues but not their pay, as well as among working mothers, who felt forced, like Santa, into playing too many "positions" at once. Santa also attracted the very fans long thought lost to basketball and football: disaffected young people who loved to watch Santa haul ass all over the diamond, chasing down pop flies or running after routine grounders that went for doubles or triples or inside-the-park home runs with Santa trying to cover the entire field. Tonight these "street youths" had been especially boisterous in the early innings, shouting instructions, mocking Santa as the score became more and more lopsided. But by the fifth inning or so, a more introspective mood had taken hold. They spoke more respectfully about his abilities, admired his pluck and inexhaustible energy. They got into lengthy discussions with nearby working mothers and office stiffs about life's difficulties. A thoughtful youth had turned to another in his crew and said, "That's how it is, you know what I'm saying?" as Santa chugged after a base-clearing roller into right field. "Just me against the whole world," he murmured.

Now among these fans there was a quickening of hope, and Santa himself felt as he hadn't felt in years. Oh, to round the bases an infinite number of times, he thought. Oh, to be everywhere again.

He proceeded to have a rally unprecedented in the history of the sport. He seemed to shake off the laws of physics. His confidence fed on itself. It was the only energy he knew that could create energy. He couldn't have said exactly where his body was at any given moment, yet his body knew exactly what to do. The crowd noise melded into a continuous roar. His elves were keening en masse now. They seemed ready to serve him again.

The score was 43–30 when something pierced Santa's reverie of complete offensive efficiency. It was the third-base umpire hesitating for a fraction of a second over a call. Finally his arms swept horizontally—safe! The third baseman went nose to nose with the ump, vociferating madly.

For his part, Santa was mystified, standing on second base,

breathing deeply yet without a sense of oxygen deficit. Surely that imaginary Santa should have been easily safe at third. In fact, Santa was a little surprised the runner hadn't tried to score. Were the simulations underestimating him? He couldn't blame them, for he had never felt this good on the playing field before. He wondered if this was a last heroic gasp on the part of his central nervous system, a sort of hot flash, heralding the menopause of his powers. Yet the surge itself, whatever its source, was undeniable. The game was getting within his reach, but he had to persuade the umps to redo his simulation variables.

He jogged back to the batter's box, while the second-base umpire and the third-base umpire tried to calm down the Cubs manager and third baseman. There would be an ejection any second, Santa could feel it. The crowd wasn't booing yet, but there was a nervous exasperated energy in the air mixed with the sort of anticipation that permeates a ballpark when records are being set. Santa got the ear of the home-plate umpire and said, "I feel good."

"You're the one, the only," the ump said sardonically.

"I haven't felt this good in years. I not only beat that throw to third easily, I could have scored."

"Just be glad your imaginary friends aren't so reckless," the umpire laughed.

"Can I be tested again? Right now? I think I'm in a zone."

The ump didn't respond, apparently absorbed in the rhubarb at third base. The third baseman kicked dirt at the third-base umpire who had turned his back on him. The second-base umpire promptly ejected the third baseman from the game. The manager protested. He was gesturing with his right hand, poking it forward, jabbing with his index finger, dangerously close to the second-base umpire's chest.

"You don't believe me, do you?" Santa said.

"Look, to be honest, I think they gave you the benefit of the doubt on your seventh-inning numbers. You didn't look good, Santa."

"I know. I didn't feel good either. But I feel better now. I feel unreal now."

"Sure, sure. There's no provision for it."

"You're the home-plate ump. It's your game. Make a provision."

The Cubs manager actually did poke the second-base umpire in the chest and was also ejected.

"Look, Santa, the rules are the rules, even for a bright boy like yourself." The home-plate ump stepped away and shouted at the lingering Cubs manager: "Hey, you're outta here! Play ball! Play ball!"

Santa stepped back into the box. The conversation with the umpire had done something to his concentration. He recognized his surroundings again. He was back in the ballpark, back in his body, back in normal space-time. There was only one thing to do: be patient, be precise, hit it where they ain't.

On the next pitch, Santa poked a base hit into left field. And slowly he built his momentum again, keeping his baserunning calls on the conservative side. He was flawless at the plate, but having to rein himself in on the base paths somehow exerted a drag on his overall level of confidence. The score was 43–38.

The Cubs called for yet another reliever, Pedro Benavídez, a fireballing journeyman with control issues. He would have to do most of his warm-up on the mound. The crowd was on its feet, weary, amazed. It was 1:00 Sunday morning. The game should have been called due to lateness. The fans should have left, but nobody would leave now. This was baseball history, and Cubs fans could appreciate it, even if it came at their expense.

Santa spoke to the ump again: "Have you ever seen anyone play this way before?"

"What would the kids think if Santa broke the rules?" the ump said.

Then Santa had an inspiration. "How about a Christmas carol?" Santa asked. Part of the charm of a Santa game was the way he would break into Christmas carols in between innings or during a lull in the action. The microphone used for the national anthem was kept available in the host team's dugout for just such a purpose. It was in Santa's contract. The ump nodded reluctantly. While Benavídez trotted in from the bull pen, Santa headed over to the Cubs' dugout.

"Hey, fellas, the microphone?"

The Cubs told Santa exactly what he could do with the microphone, yet no one stopped him when he picked up the stand, which was still plugged into its jack, and pulled it onto the field. At this sign that Santa was going to sing, a mixed roar went up from the crowd. Their fascination and disgust with Santa had never been more intense.

Santa flicked the "on" switch and blew into the microphone. A breeze whistled through the stadium. The crowd hushed.

"Ladies and gentlemen," Santa said, "I'd like to pass the time by singing a holiday favorite, but first let me say a few words. Folks, I *am* Santa Claus. No matter what happens during the rest of this game, I want you to know that. I know that some of you still think I'm just a publicity stunt. But at one time I planned, supervised, and executed the greatest production and distribution network the world has ever seen!"

His voice went up on this last point, but there was almost no applause. Some of Santa's Helpers cheered, but all were shushed by their comrades who didn't want to miss a word of Santa's speech.

"And if you only believed, I'd still be delivering those gifts." This prompted scattered bursts of heckling. Santa felt the fans slipping away from him. "Look, I'm only asking you to believe what you've seen with your own eyes. Isn't it obvious that I'm playing better than I've ever played before? Ladies and gentlemen, as you well know, a simulator dictates how the Santas on-base will perform. I have good reason to believe that the simulator is currently underestimating my abilities. I am better than anyone can imagine right now, and I'd like to prove it by asking the umpires to retest me and to recalibrate the simulator. What do you think? Wouldn't that be fair, to recalibrate the simulator?"

The crowd's response was mixed. There were thousands of isolated yells and cheers and hecklings. Mothers and overburdened office workers called for fairness. Traditionalists and impatient children—as well as some of Santa's stressed out, overly-empathetic fans—called for a speedy end to the game.

Meanwhile, as Benavídez continued his warm-up tosses, the umpires gathered near home plate, alarmed at this turn in Santa's presentation. A few Cubs players hovered nearby, arguing that Santa be silenced, but this only delayed the umpires' deliberations. The second-base umpire noted that, technically, Santa was allowed to "entertain the crowd" at such a moment, which prompted the Cubs, who were panicking at the prospect of being the first team to lose to Santa, to demand a definitive ruling from the commissioner. One of the umps ran to the Cubs' dugout, picked up a brace of cell phones, and came back out on the field. There was a delay because the commissioner was asleep—in the sort of deep unreachable sleep that only prescription sleep medications can produce—and it took some time to get the commissioner coherent and ready to answer the umpires' question.

"What do you all say?" Santa asked through the microphone. How many of you think I *shouldn't* be allowed to redo the variables?"

A cheer went up from the crowd.

"All right, how many of you think I *should* be allowed to redo the variables?"

Some say the second cheer was stronger.

"And this is a Cubs crowd," Santa shouted off-mike to the umpires who had paused their discussion to watch Santa's appeal.

The home-plate umpire glared at Santa and threw down his cell phone. Santa's insolence had crossed a line. He stormed over to where Santa stood, snatched the microphone from his hand, turned it off, and ejected Santa from the game.

Santa was thunderstruck.

"You're ejecting me? Santa Claus? Jolly old Saint Nick? You're ejecting *me?* How dare you!"

"Pack it in, Santa," the ump said without raising his voice. "You got the mike on false pretenses. That's a violation."

They went back and forth for a bit, but the ump was implacable. Santa mastered his rage; there was still a possibility.

"If you won't let me play, at least let me redo the simulator."

"Why should I let you redo the simulator? You're out of here! The game's over!"

Santa patiently reminded the ump about his pinch hitter, the Santa Machine, and how it could bat in his place if he was ejected, and how this made it worth redoing the simulations for the base runners.

"Screw your simulations," the ump said, though Santa could tell he was remembering the never-used pinch hitter. "You're out of the game." He pointed to Santa's dugout.

There was nothing Santa could do. The ump's decision was beyond appeal. But before he left the field, Santa signaled a substitution to the simulator ump. He was to be replaced at the plate by the Mercury MicroRobotics Inc. Santa Machine batter apparatus.

Now the crowd really wanted to leave, but something held

it there, fascinated against its will. Santa was being ejected, but, hey, the game wasn't over. The ground crew wheeled a bright-red contraption onto the field. It was a complex system of metal, rubber, cameras, levers, springs, motors, hydraulics, and microprocessors, mounted on a wide base, the wheels of which the crew was locking down. The Santa Machine was activated. It took a few practice swings. The crowd's murmuring hushed for a second, then redoubled: the path of the swing was unmistakable. And when the Santa Machine crooned "play ball, play ball," in something very much like Santa's own voice, a wave of excitement passed through the stands.

Meanwhile, Santa headed slowly back to his dugout and the swarm of agitated elves. He was completely humiliated. It reminded him of his first betrayal as Santa Claus: when the Gang of Seven industrialists who first bankrolled him decided how to market him. The reality of his operation was fantastic enough, but these archcapitalists wanted nothing more than to obscure this reality in favor of the Santa legend we have come to know: one overloaded sleigh, eight flying reindeer, rooftop landings, down the chimney. That was all very quaint. It was production and distribution without infrastructure, without decimated forests or gaping strip mines, belching steamers or coal-burning trains; without a race of elves who knew nothing of a regular wage, who had been relocated by the tens of thousands to factories and courier posts overseas, who had surrendered their will to the Alpha Craftsman, a hyperkinetic taskmaster with a meglomaniacal twinkle in his eye. That damned marketing plan was his first inkling that bastards somehow larger than himself were really in control.

And there were his mad elves crowding the mesh screen. A few, without seeming to notice Santa's approach, poured forth obscenities and complaints against him. Gundt Angleford, who normally kept a filthy parchment tightly rolled and inserted down the front of his green flannel pants, now read from the scroll in a monotonous, high-pitched voice, listing the names of elves who had died in the civil war. What comfort could Santa offer? He had already promised them too much—to play alongside him in this great American game (the commissioner, they now knew, had nixed that), to sit in a convoy of limousines during his victory parade (Santa had told them he would dominate the league), even endorsement contracts (unfortunately the elves' rapacious grins made them unsuitable representatives for most products)—and his promises had gone unfulfilled.

Fishing out the screen-door key, Santa was so lost in these thoughts he didn't notice the Santa Machine lash a crisp single into right field, scoring an imaginary runner. A good number of elves still clung to the mesh, hanging on by their long, yellow fingernails, entranced, seemingly blind to the difference between him and the apparatus. With Ube Trindle and Dinker Underdale following dejectedly behind him, he unlocked the screen door and stepped into verbal mayhem:

"Get back to work!"

"You abused us!"

"We made you!"

"What is this shit!"

"Ejected!"

"Easy now," Santa said. "Easy." He couldn't help but eye in passing the runway to the clubhouse, an escape, but there were six or seven silent elves on the threshold, blocking the way, morosely smoking hand-rolled cigarettes and staring at him with hooded eyes. Another elf silently wrapped his body around Santa's left shin, clinging to him like an enormous boot, making him walk stiff-legged while looking for a relatively calm spot on the bench. The air in the dugout was fetid, stifling, and Santa began to sweat like he never had on the field.

"Global distribution network!" an elf cried.

"Production synergies!" another screamed.

Someone was pounding a bat against a concrete wall. It made a sickening sound. Santa looked to see who it was, to give the order to stop it, but there were too many roiling elf bodies in the way—one hanging from a light fixture, another standing on the water cooler, several riding on a partner's shoulders.

"The trains, the trains!"

"Get back to work!"

"We're doomed. We'll never make it."

"What about our emotions!" one male elf suddenly cried. It was Ube Trindle. "What about our feelings!"

Santa stopped trying to move past the elves who surrounded him.

"Emotions?" Santa said. "Feelings?"

"You never loved us, Santa!" This was Dinker Underdale. "You never did."

Santa could not make himself look into her glittering eyes.

"He never loved us!"

"No love! No love!"

"Loved you?" Santa said, half to himself. Then he raised his voice. "Of course I loved you. Didn't you feel it? You were my elves. We produced and distributed together! Greater love hath no man than this, that a man organize the production and—"

But Santa was drowned out by new cries from the other side of the dugout:

"Distribute!"

"Destroy!"

"Distribute!"

"Destroy!"

With these words, the rallying cries of the two sides in the civil war—the traditionalists who would return to the good old days of toy destruction, and the Santa loyalists who would carry on the global distribution network—the situation threatened to get out of control. Dinker Underdale raised her voice over the melee, using the slogan that had once united the elves: "But distribution *is* destruction!" she yelled. "Destruction is distribution!" Yet at these words the roiling of the elves only intensified; a second bat began thunking against the wall, keeping time with the first.

The Santa apparatus smashed a double off the wall in right center and stood at home plate, upright and poised, while imaginary Santas toured the bases and the crowd roared. Meanwhile certain elves began to pinch and tear Santa's outfit with their long, yellow fingernails. A strip of thermal undershirt ripped free, Santa's pale flesh was exposed, fingernails struck again, blood was drawn, and at the sight of Santa's blood, the elves went berserk. Some scratched rapidly at his body with two hands, like rodents digging holes, while others swarmed his limbs and lifted him off his feet. They furiously pulled and jerked and scratched and tore and twisted and smashed until Santa suddenly came apart—all at once, like a barn struck by a tornado—and was distributed throughout his dugout.

In the aftermath, the elves reeled about as if drunk, wiping their red fingernails on their green pants. Many of them, howling and moaning, piled down the runway to the clubhouse. Soon every shower in the locker room was running, and the scent of strawberry Herbal Essence body wash wafted through the corridors and into the dugout.

Meanwhile the rally of the imaginary Santas went on. The network TV cameras portrayed only close-ups and replays of the amazing Santa apparatus and the run-scoring imaginary Santas, and thus the scene in the dugout was not broadcast, nor could it have been clearly observed because of the elves still hanging on the mesh to watch the game, and so virtually no one in the stadium was aware of what had happened to Santa. The Santa simulation was in complete harmony with itself, and by singles and doubles, it methodically erased the Cubs' lead. The fans buried their faces in their hands, or danced in the aisles, or stared, unbearably nervous, at the scoreboard, which read 43–42. A runner had advanced to third on a futile throw home. Still two out.

Benavídez prowled behind the mound in an impotent rage, massaging a new baseball as if he would flatten it between his hands. Finally he retoed the rubber, a flat, hard look in his eyes.

The imaginary Santa on third took an egregious lead. Would Santa try to steal home? That didn't seem right.

But Benavídez ignored the runner. He went into his full windup, reared back, and threw a fastball at the head of the Santa Machine—which ducked just as the catcher sprang up like a jack-in-the-box to glove the malicious pitch. The catcher pump-faked a throw to third, and the imaginary Santa dove safely back to the bag. Santa's Helpers booed angrily, and the "Santa = Genocide" banner rippled in the stadium lights.

Some of the elves remaining in the dugout shrieked approval, while a glassy-eyed Dinker Underdale wandered aimlessly among Santa's scattered remains.

The umpire should have cautioned Benavídez, but, strangely, this did not happen.

Then the Santa Machine whiffed on a wicked forkball, and Benavídez seemed to take heart. He decided to challenge the apparatus with his fastball. He put every last bit of mustard on that pitch. The Santa Machine put a beautiful swing on it and struck a soaring shot to dead center field that cleared the wall by forty feet and thudded into the simulator screen that had been displaying its flight. The imaginary Santa on third danced down the line with his arms over his head, jumping the last yard and landing with both feet together on home plate, while the imaginary Santa batter rounded the bases, forefinger raised high. And just like that, to the crowd's relief and amazement, the imaginary Santas had won the game, 44–43.

Only at that moment did Santa's career stats become eternally fixed. As a pitcher, and as a player, his mark was 1-323, though in the record books there is an asterisk next to the "1." The corresponding note reads: "Game won while dead."

Every year, the Santa simulation team interrupts a regular league game to play a memorial "inning at bat," not on Memorial Day, but on the Fourth of July. And at the very end of the postgame fireworks display, through the dark smoky sky so recently lit with explosions, an airplane pulls a long balloon contraption on which are arranged lights that form an image of eight flying reindeer, an enormous sleigh filled with toys, and Santa in the driver's seat. His lighted arm waves mechanically. His electric face is dazzling. The crowd applauds and goes home.

Acknowledgments

Thanks to everyone who gave me helpful feedback on these stories, especially Mark Wisniewski, Lisa Lenzo, Bonnie Jo Campbell, Glenn Deutsch, Mike Stefaniak, Lorri Alberts, Carla Vissers, Jenica Moore, Nick Benca, George Dila, Josie Kearns, John Mauk, Phillip Sterling, Julia Hanna, Mary Winifred Hood, Jeff Schwaner, Annie Gilson, Bruce Mills, Scott Haycock, and Jayne Anne Phillips. Thanks to Annie Martin and all of the great folks at Wayne State who have provided me with every comfort of a literary home. I would also like to thank Kalamazoo College and Writers in the Heartland for their support during the writing of these stories. Finally, thanks to my parents and my brothers and sisters for giving me a secure place to stand and to Lorri and Madeleine for, well, everything.

I am also grateful to the editors at the magazines in which these stories first appeared, sometimes in somewhat different form: "Dogs I Have Known" in *The Missouri Review;* "Pelvis" (originally as "Hips") in *Mississippi Review;* "Overpass" in *The Southern Review;* "Proofreader" in *Phoebe;* "Séance" (originally as "She Was Moist") in *Stet* and *Del Sol Review;* "A Talented Individual" in *Natural Bridge;* "Helmet of Ice" in *Quarterly West;* "Quality Snacks" in *River Styx;* "Self-Reliance" in *Nerve;* "Woman of Peace" (originally appeared as "The BBs") in *Joyland*; "My Nonsexual Affair" in *Ecotone;* "Windows Reflect Some Light" and "Always the Same Dream" in *DIAGRAM;* "The Bad Reader" in *The Brooklyner;* "No Joy in Santa's Village" in *The Small Chair* (*McSweeney's* iPhone app).